PURSUE
GOOD

(Noted - previous edition name of the book is "Leo's Focus Towards a Better Life")

Is it possible to endeavour to live a 100% and beyond, better standard of living?

Is there a chance of finding a better partner? Is it possible to face no divorce?

L Can you have better educated children? **L**

With the possibility of a better life?

Is there the potential for very good health, whiter teeth,

I maybe no cancer, healthy organs, **I**

A focus on smiling and laughter?

F Happiness? **F**

!!!!

E !! **E**

!

C U P Are you the **potential owner of a great life?** C U P

This book may be worth its weight in gold.

Suresh Thakrar

Could the difference between Without and With "Pursue Twice as Good a Life" book take to following possibilities?

<u>From a Young Age</u>

Motivation Lift	Without the book May be, -Very Good Life -Good Life -Bad Life	<u>With "Pursue twice as good a life" Book</u> <u>Choose your Life Scheme</u> and <u>Work towards that.</u> <u>May be</u> <u>-VERY GOOD LIFE</u> <u>-TWICE AS GOOD A LIFE</u> <u>-YOUR CHOICE LIFE</u>

Is it not worth using "Motivation Lift" as best as possible to see if youngster's life can be "Twice as Good"?

Author's Note

All the texts should be referred to as reading matter and any actions taken by youngsters, parents, other people and professionals, are done so on their own full legal recognisance and risk. All the parents or adults, when referring to any matters regarding minors in this book, do so on their own legal recognisance and risk.

The readers of this book are advised to seek help and advice from appropriate professionals, like doctors, counsellors, consultants, dentists, psychologists and physiotherapists on all the matters of physical exercises, human organs and all other health matters. This book does not give authoritative advice on health, mental health, longevity, finance and all other subjects where professional advice needs to be sought from suitably qualified professionals.

There is some content that is repeated again and again to act as reminders for the readers themselves or to help remind others and the readers' forbearance is asked for and appreciated. Again, the readers must seek advice from appropriate professionals as needed.

The author, copyright owner, publishers, translators or distributors cannot be held legally or in any other manner, responsible in any way.

It is noted that this book is a new edition of "Leo's Focus Towards a Better Life" book being produced. It is noted that the name of the book is changed to "Pursue Twice as Good a Life". Also, additional texts have been added.

ISBN; 978-1-7393544-3-5

Why buy "Pursue Twice as Good a Life" book? Some of the following details could well be used as **Motivational Lift**:

1) Up to and beyond "Twice as Good a Life" may follow for you and your youngster when you take some details from this book and select options that can be acted on.
2) The book can guide you to help your child understand important details about good studies, organised-disciplined living and working out good ways to "Not Spend Money" and "Spend Money", when appropriate.
3) Maintaining very good health and attaining twice good salary scales as best as possible.
4) Learning to reject all potential bad addictions as best as possible.
5) Potential for no divorce nor separation possibilities to be examined.
6) For accommodation, achieving double the size of the house and being able to afford the own choice car.
7) Lots and lots more to understand and use, on offer!

Information:
Email: info@pursueagoodlife.com

Introduction

The front cover of the book is almost as good as the introduction.

By reading this book, there may be potential for up to and beyond 100% improvement in standard of living, progressing good life with good trimmings like what Leo has been able to achieve. Better than expected some very desired aspects of happy life are possible when some texts are considered and adopted to one's own needs and circumstances. Correct efforts can potentially lead to filling own and family members' good life cup desires with many needs like good bank balance, spacious living accommodation, good car and own choice other needs. Why not potentially conquer good health, whiter healthier teeth, less possibility of separation or divorce if living with a partner and better educated, more mature, happier children over time as the person/people may well have own children. One can continue all the good that the individual/ family are doing and adopting some extra good points that are appropriate, adding good efforts that can help win the good happy life cup scenarios better with increased frequency.

A person needs to know a little bit about various terms such as counting, being civil, what health issues to react to, lots of learning on happenings around one and happiness, in general. Counting is one of those essentials which helps one in managing your own money and focuses the mind on payment of rent or mortgages, as may be applicable. Hopefully, whilst counting some more, one learns to live within one's means and survive. Being civil is home-grown talent where, as well as being polite, one may consider remaining on the right side of the law. And why not – instinctively we know what of our own health issues to react to and when needed, we take a doctor's advice. Doctors, when prompted, may well advise on very good physical exercises that the individual should do to hopefully minimise visits to the doctor. Good health may then prevail, for the individual. Learning from birth, blessed with the help of one or two parents, who could be counted as the best teachers, help the baby to grow up whilst learning how to survive and prosper. Perhaps little baby instinctively knows when the baby is happy. Could the baby be helped to continue to learn to be happier? The contribution of teachers to help toddlers, children and youngsters to keep on learning all through the years is worthy of very high praise. Good conditioning of one's thoughts may help control emotions and needs to be taught so that things are managed better. Learning to spend too much money, falling prey to addictions and ignoring good lessons when one should have attended to them, are not boundaries worth crossing. The big question is how quickly and efficiently could living a life be substantially improved? How does an improvement in living standards of up to a hundred percent or more, sound?

The efficiency of any adventure, when demonstrated with incredible success in whatever field, can potentially be somewhat replicated in real life. I had the biggest disappointment in my life in 1970 when my father died at the age of 58. I was then aged 19 and had no house to live in in Uganda because my father's family accommodation was provided on the basis that he needed to continue to work for a company. No house and almost no money meant that the only option we had at the time was to go to India with my mother, 2 younger brothers and a young sister. Fortunately, we did have a house in a rural village in India that my father had bought some years prior, so at least, we had a roof over our heads. I had suffered previous setbacks when I lost three years of studies because of the change from English to Gujarati medium and back to English medium education. This time, I wanted to stick to English medium studies and we had to go and rent a flat in another town. Thereafter, I passed my senior secondary school exams and further to that, passed my first year science in college in Mumbai. Additionally, I did a 5 years' degree course in metallurgical engineering in Baroda and graduated with a Bachelor of Engineering (Metallurgy) with first-class distinction. That did pay off as I reduced castings' defects in my first job by about two thousand percent. My main focus all these years from 1970 to 1977 was education. At that time, I had to take care of my illiterate mother and also help my younger siblings as much as possible. The situation improved slightly between 1974 and 1977 because I had managed to get permission to send my mother and siblings to the UK to join my elder brothers who had settled there after expulsion by Idi Amin in Uganda. I am very grateful to my elder brothers and more grateful to my younger siblings who actually started working in factories to provide funds for me to continue my education in India. The important point to make here is that from ages 19 to 26 there were no other distractions apart from studies and a will to survive.

Collecting my thoughts on about two-thousand percent reduction in defects in castings as stated earlier, my focus on the hope to helping people improve their standards of living is not modest. But I propose a massive improvement in standard of living. The hopes here are to help improve your quality of life by up to a hundred percent or more, if possible. Parents trying to improve the living standard of children in the future can aim to improve their average living standard by up to hundred percent, or more, when the children are grown up. The children spend a number of years studying, where the time can be well spent preparing for perfection in improving living standards in the future. An adult person at the age of thirty trying to improve their current living standard from this point on has to start from now and so has less time to do that. Maybe one learns some things as time goes along and when reading this book some details can be seen that one can use now or sometime in the future – that is worth making at least a mental note of. On the final analysis, it is always the individual's choice what gets used and what does not.

The author is very humble in his approach and does not want to dictate suggestions to anyone. There is a good wish for every one and whatever path they choose is their own privilege and responsibility. The author wishes everyone a good, happy life.

The world today is what people have made the world to be and there are great things that have been achieved. Whatever the deficiencies, some children are exposed to the sharp end of some of those shortcomings. For many children, the overall aim is to substantially improve their standards of living. Giving them proper guidance can help make a huge positive difference. Some practices had adverse effects on children and youngsters. They now need good guidance and practices to help them to change that around to a good difference. The parents and teachers are doing a wonderful job of trying to improve children's standards as much as possible. Leo, an imaginary child, and his approach and practices can help guide readers to look at good options. Some of these can be adopted to assist in making potential improvements for everyone, including children. The children and youngsters, some of whom unknowingly sacrifice chunks of their good future on being 'cool' may wish to consider details suggested in this book. One could choose a wonderful, long, healthy, wealthy and happy life that can progress to a good old age, when a number of things are put right from the start. A potential of up to 100% or more, better living, on average, takes on 'good cool living 'til a very old age'. Mature folks can join the crusade to enrich their lives that hopefully also get better. Many may find their own means of helping children and youngsters improve immensely. On average, being 'cool at a very young age' can well be translated to 'being immensely cool, all through one's life, and raising a cool family' may follow.

If I could ask you a simple question: If by reading a book and implementing a number of measures, procedures and actions that you approve, you or your child's life can have a chance to improve by up to a hundred percent or more –almost doubling your current standard of living –would you seriously read that book? This is that book.

Pursue Twice as Good Life

Contents

Chapter 1

Introducing Leo

The front cover of this book highlights the Gold Cup with the name of the book "Pursue Twice as Good a Life" which can be considered as a Life Cup. That even directs one to take that to be for the future potential owner of a great life. At the start, all that can incorporate imaginary smiles from the individuals or the parent/s. Pursue twice as good a life suggests very good health, wealth, twice a good living standard and other areas of enhancements, wherever possible. Achieving up to and beyond, one hundred percent improvement in good living standard needs to be the target. For that to happen, the individuals and the parent/s need to continue doing whatever they have been doing, but select the ideas, methods and tricks that they identify as helpful after reading this book, and apply them according to their choice. The approach here is to incorporate their own knowledge and use that to help themselves or a baby, toddler, or child to progress as much as possible. This book will speak of the imaginary parent/s of the imaginary child Leo, who are going to bring up Leo and demonstrate how he could do almost everything, right from the start. I refer to 'parent/s' instead of parent or parents to show that there could well be one or two parents who are bringing up Leo. Leo is a boy but there is an acknowledgement that human life as a person is one of the biggest achievements in real life, in the world, and any person's life needs to be celebrated. Leo's parent/s dream of Leo achieving a very happy life with more than double the standard of living of that achieved by his local peers/friends from school where Leo is brought up. The parent/s are organising Leo's life in every way, as much as possible. Leo is going to demonstrate how he is going to do things from very young age, with the help of his parent/s. The project is aimed at individuals who want to improve their own lives as well as parent/s of children who want to improve their children's lives.

We pay tribute to the sporting events with the view to focus on champions getting the winning cups and the necessity for sports which promote physical exercises. It is well known that children, youngsters and people who do regular, good physical exercise maintain excellent health to a very old age.

The front page can also be accepted as a Life Cup challenge and throws down a gauntlet, asking who is going to win the Life Cup, and to what extent? Imagine how emotions run high when football teams' aspiration is to play with endurance – there is a kind of exuberance and excitement invlived for players and observers alike. Or there is the potential of a complete disappointment. The Life Cup challenge is for life and real endurance is constantly challenged by own thoughts, conscious choices and the desire to get life right without making bad mistakes. In the Life Cup, the greatest number of wins are the sizes and the quality of life wins on scales that one can decide for oneself. It is very important to take ownership and cleverly work very hard for years to be a truly happy, healthy and wealthy individual. Then one can appreciate the good fortune being earned, enjoyed and appreciated to the full.

One may up the stakes and allocate a Life Cup prize to the toddler for successfully passing nursery schooling and wishing them good luck in primary school. The same procedure can be repeated when the child leaves the primary school and goes to secondary school. No cash gift needs to be given to the toddler or a child as the combination of cash money and a young age can cause lots of problems and potential bad habits in real life. It is ultimately the parent/s responsibility but it is not worth taking any chances for the youngsters to get hold of cash. The child can look forward to entrance to primary schooling and then to secondary schooling. These are good hopes and further steps to basic good learning that can form a foundation to a secure basic education.

Some people like to read numbered instructions. Some people like a kind of story-telling format and one can learn a lot from that. This book is kind of story-telling format to help one to take some and leave some details, as per own choice. There are numbered points from time to time as well. Could you choose to take one or maybe a large percentage of the good advice that is provided here? Reading the messages in the story-like format has been made interesting for people to enjoy. Learning a number of new ways to do things, one may follow some points and may wish to ignore other points.

One can pinpoint the actual standard of living for a particular person on a specific date and at a level as a measurable point to be recorded. What can that individual do to improve their standard of living by up to fifty or indeed, a hundred percent? Focussing on up to one hundred percent improvement, one needs to imagine doubling the standard of living. The doubling of the standard of living is in no way a ceiling and further improvements are indeed desirable and possible.

The focus needs to be placed where a substantial improvement in standard of living can happen. It is noted that, on average, people do try to improve their standard of living. The focus of this book is to achieve an *accelerated* improvement in standard of living. For this to be considered, one needs to look at two groups of individuals. From the first group is one adult person living and working in this world. The individual's age is assumed to be thirty years. This person is living, enjoying a particular standard of living. The question for this person is, how long is it going to take for this person to achieve up to one-hundred percent improvement in their standard of living? After reading this book, this person intends making changes to help accelerate, improvements in standard of living.

An individual considered from a second group is an imaginary baby named Leo who is recently born. Having been born in a particular imaginary family in a particular city like London, Leo is expected to do the normal things like study for many years and then start working, attaining a particular standard of living. That standard of living would be comparable to most of Leo's peer group or friends, in the future. The previous experience can point to the average living standard Leo can expect, having been brought up in the local situation, with the facilities and efforts that are normally put in by average parent/s. The youngsters in an average peer group are achieving a particular average life standard of living that is marked as one hundred points. This will help to clarify further on, the improvements in standard of living.

Leo's imaginary parent/s are not satisfied with all that and want Leo to achieve up to an average of two hundred points life standard of living. That is meant to be up to double the average standard of living that the parent/s want Leo to achieve. This book's focus is directed mainly to Leo's life until old age, and evaluating if he can achieve two hundred points, or double the average standard of living.

Any child or person joining at the age of nine or twenty or thirty or forty-four and not from birth, would have had a late start to improving the average standard of living. For an adult, the average improvement in standard of living can only be measured from the date that that individual's efforts in that direction have started. A very important point in this adventure of improving the standard of living by up to a hundred percent to almost doubling the standard of living, remains the focus for everyone who is interested in this quest. A better standard of living could stretch to improvement in education, health, wealth, job, salary, and so on. Leo needs to be able to control his temper very well and needs to develop the habit of living well within his means. Safety needs to be important to Leo and he hopes to be able to live enjoying double the standard of living in the future.

Leo has twenty-five years of good support, full living expenses paid, huge responsibilities to behave, achieve excellent studies and gain an amazing amount of understanding of life. One other important thing that Leo must do is be happy from inside. Fortunately, Leo has learnt that from a very young age and in general, he is almost always happy. Leo must and wants to, reject addictions like smoking cigarettes, drinking too much alcohol, taking on bad gambling and use of drugs. Also, Leo would understand good rules set by his parent/s regarding disciplined study times, homework, revision of lessons, planning for the following day's lessons and so on. Leo knows that he could be rewarded with maybe double or triple the average salary for the following forty or fifty years, after graduating from university.

Late joiners in the quest for improvement in standard of living, may start at any age. The main focus is placed on Leo's life from birth onwards so that improvement in life can be looked at from birth to very old age. Any late comer in this quest, having read the whole book, would hopefully know how to apply the improvements in living a life too.

Human nature dictates that when something is good, and can be legally adopted/used, then a person would not only let it happen but would embrace it. Any individual reading "Pursue Twice as Good a Life" and adopting many of the ways and means of improving their own life and the lives of their own family members, may consider improving life to whatever extent that may be possible. The whole book is written in the context of an imaginary child Leo and from baby stage, the life he lives is stretched to a good living age where almost all the desired ambitions are exceeded by Leo. While up to one hundred percent improvement in average quality of life is looked at, there is nothing stopping someone else from improving the quality of their own life by say thirty percent to, one hundred percent, in a number of years. You can use your own version of tricks that are written about in this book as best as possible. Very good results may be possible. After 100% improvement in standard of living is achieved, there is nothing stopping the individual from further improvements in standard of living, if that is possible. The book would have an appeal to most people who are open to the possibility of improving their own lives as well as the lives of their family members.

The parent/s, are a hundred percent carers for the child and would be wise not to let go some significant percentage of the full own carer influence and privilege on the child. Many good friends of the child also help the child a lot by allowing the child to learn from peer group friends. Some friends could be bad influence at times on the child, however. The child could learn to spend a lot of time watching television or listening to music when that time should have been spent studying. The parent/s need to be the parents, as well as, kind of, the child's best friend/s, as much as possible. That does not mean the parent/s' good discipline that is in the child's interest can be allowed to slip away. All the parent/s' good deeds need to be done whether the child is in a state school or in a private school. It is very much preferable for the parent/s to spend a lot of time with the child, although it is noted that that can be very difficult. Parent/s helping with school work, homework, planning for the lessons of the following day, reading books, explaining difficulties in life when the child is the right age, are all very important tasks for the parent/s.

It is appropriate that the child, at some stage, could take their own responsibility for themselves on a full-time basis. It is a wonderful and happy occasion for the parent when the child is clever, educated, healthy and mature enough to safely, happily live independently in this world.

Imaginary baby Leo's life journey is explained all the way from being born, to growing up during the educational years, entering the working life, and beyond. Yes, there are claims made and repeated that Leo has never smoked cigarettes, never got into habit of drinking too much alcohol and so on. Yes, Leo has kept almost all the so-called very bad habits or addictions away from his own life. Leo has continued doing good physical exercises which has kept him in very good health. If any adults want to look at any of these details to help their own children choose a good path or even help make small changes in their own lives and seek medical help, as may be needed, it is their choice.

It is a well-known fact that after certain age, people have the right to choose what they do in their lives, like smoking cigarettes, drinking too much alcohol, engaging in bad gambling, and so on. Some people also use drugs at their own risk. It is not the intention of the author to criticise anyone choosing to do these things. People have many rights and freedom to do what they want to do, at their own risk. Even the activities like living beyond one's means are the choices some people make. Some people may be unwilling to control their temper, and so on. It is important not to consider one sentence or a paragraph in isolation and consider a topic in isolation. Overall aims need to be considered and the concepts in the book are to help people, if possible, not judge them.

There are very important issues and regrettably, some of the very common mistakes made by some people need to be tackled. There are very many repetitions in this book mainly to emphasize again and again to encourage the reader to do the right things. Also, repetitions are meant to be reminders not to adopt some bad habits if possible.

Up to and beyond a hundred percent better life is not going to happen unless good relevant efforts are put in by the individual. It may well be appropriate to continue good efforts for life. Even when one gets a good job, it may be necessary to work hard as well as update one's skills. A child can learn about good efforts from parent/s and teachers. At some stage, one may well need to take the responsibility and decide on what good work that needs to be done. Not all people can be successful. Some people sometimes cannot get the jobs that they would like. A very few people, even after good qualifications, find it difficult to get the jobs that they would like. It needs to be understood that many people with very good qualifications are able to find good work that they like. Sometimes, it takes a short time and other times it takes a long time for some people to find work. Perhaps a good thing to do is not to lose patience. One may be able to find some other work that is not related to the qualifications that one has achieved. Is it better to do some job in the short term or wait to get a better job? All these decisions and actions depend on one's own self and circumstances. One also needs to understand that getting a very good education and university degree/s does require disciplined studies that the individual needs to do, for years. That certainly gives the individual a better chance of getting a well-paid job.

Who is the best person to look after yourself? The answer could be your own self. You do know when you are hungry. You do know when you have got a headache. The idea may well be firstly to condition yourself to be happy with what you've got? That still means nothing is stopping you from the progress and extra health, wealth and happiness that can be achieved. Your own health issues are best dealt with using specialist care like a doctor's care. But when you're conditioning yourself to be happy most of the time and keep busy doing good work, there may be less chance of depression. Doing vigorous, good physical exercises after doctor's advice may help with better overall health. You can condition yourself to be happy with no or one or two holiday breaks a year.

Chapter 2

Leo's Goal is up to 100% or More Improvement in Life.

Imaginary Leo could be your best friend. You can look at details in this book that you can choose to adopt in some self-approved format and maybe, change your life to a great degree. If a child or a person wants to improve their own life by up to 100% or more, is there enough time left for you to do that? You may well be at age nine, or twenty, or thirty or forty-four or so on. One thing is for certain, you would need lots of time and effort to be able to potentially do this. If you can look at the life of a new-born imaginary child, Leo, and see how best he can improve his life potentially by up to one hundred percent or more, then one can join the process from your own perspective. Whenever double the standard of living is achieved, there is a further possibility of improving standard of living even more.

Everyone needs to know that income and expenditure are the most important money details that people need to control, as best as possible. Amounts of money coming into people's home are some things that those people try to use to improve their lives as much as possible. Control over expenditure of money is even more important, as those should not exceed the incoming amounts, in general. People are better off when "Needs" in general are attended to and less is spent on "Wants".

In life, there is great necessity to look at "Needs". Thoughts about what is wished for or desired could translate to "Wants". If you can learn to ignore your "Wants" as much as possible and just concentrate on "Needs", you may well progress rapidly towards financial independence more quickly, provided other spending habits are kept in check. The extent to which you just cater for "Needs" and keep away from "Wants" when lots of other matters are moving towards satisfactory practices of living life may well give you a significant or even a substantial edge towards success. Could looking at the following remind you time and again to do this?

Need Need Need Need Need
Need Need Need Need
Need Need Need
Need
!!!!!
!!!
!

More emphasis on Need, not Want!
Potentially Financially Better off (Within Reason)?

Focus is the word that is so very important, when it is looked at in the right context. Focus can be looked at as being the centre of attraction and also as the centre of activity. Let's simply consider a very important sequence to start with. Let's assume that a group of children being born and growing up from infancy to toddler stage and onwards, are kept very, very happy. All the facilities and needs are met by wonderful parent/s who properly attend to all the requirements like feed times, nap times, nappy-changing times, bath times and sleep times. There may be one parent raising a child, or two parents raising a child. "Parent/s" refers to either of those possibilities. These children are always greeted with a smile or laughter. When they cry or get distressed for any reason, they are always made happy with whatever techniques the individual parents can come up with. They are taught how to crawl, walk, speak and are kept as safe as possible. Let's assume that the parents are very good and send these children to good nursery and primary schools. At some stage It is assumed that these children are very happy with their lives and do understand a fair bit about 'living a life'. When asked, would these children agree to plan to live very good lives, for the rest of their lives? What would their answer be? Could the answer be a unanimous 'yes'? Could these children be made well aware of the facts that people who want to live very good lives need to focus and prepare the circumstances in which good living can happen? They do need to be reminded, perhaps every six months, on how to focus again and again, on how they can live good lives. Could they understand that they need to study very well, look after their health by doing physical exercises, learn some other things like not spending too much money and adopt some disciplines? They need to look at a number of things that they need to do well and also some of the things that they should not do at all. Do any clever children want to adopt bad habits if their focus can be kept on good studies, a good, happy life, and respect for their parents and teachers? Can these very good standards of living be achieved due to some very good rules being followed for years and years?

Leo is an imaginary child and he is assumed to be a boy. A person is a very highly cherished individual, and living a life is, in the main, a wonderful experience. It is best if some of the times, parent/s talk straight with Leo about the issues, and repeat straight talk again and again. The idea is to talk 'good talk' with Leo, with a happy face. But gradually, important content in little chunks may be added, all the time. It does not matter if Leo does not understand; repeated discussion of certain points with Leo could help the toddler to start understanding faster, perhaps.

Is it possible to see how clever a fifteen-month-old Leo happened to be? The imaginary toddler concept is continued by adding some other imaginary characters like Leo's grandmother. Leo's grandmother was feeding him blueberries, whilst talking with him. Leo loved every minute when the grandmother fed the toddler and talked with him at the same time. When the blueberries in the dish are finished, the grandmother looked at Leo and said, "Finished," pointing to the empty dish. She also repeatedly turns her both hands upside down and said, "No more," and kept on repeating, "No more." Leo got up, took hold of grandmother's finger and walked the grandmother to the fridge in the kitchen. Leo pointed his finger to the fridge, as if to say, "More in there, more in there." Needless to say, Leo got more blueberries to eat.

The toddlers generally have a very short span of interest, but they love every minute that we spend with them. Why not form an extra hour's teaching habit at home, starting from toddler age and carried on by the parent/s throughout their education? The toddlers love our happy faces. Lots of smiles and laughs with them are very happy occasions. With safety in mind, small episodes of hide-and-seek games that we play with them makes them very happy.

Toddler Leo started developed extra naughty behaviour when aged around eighteen months, but the parent/s did not mind that at this stage. The parent/s would allow naughty behaviour happily not forgetting to smile as much as possible. The distraction techniques worked very well. Toddler Leo, assumed to be clever, would be naughty and the parent/s would tell him what wrong had been done by him and he had to say sorry. Toddler Leo would say sorry. The parent/s would smile and pick up Leo and cuddle the toddler. The parent/s started noticing that toddler Leo would do the same naughty deed so that after a little confrontation with the parent, he would say sorry and get a big smile and a cuddle. Leo liked and loved the ‘smile and cuddle rewards’ that he would be naughty in the same manner again, and again. The parent/s being very clever picked up on this. Leo would be deliberately naughty so that after saying sorry, he would get a nice smile and a cuddle. The parent/s changed the technique so that when Leo became naughty, the parent/s would confront him and make him say sorry. Now, Leo had to add that he would not do that particular naughty behaviour again. Also, on these occasions, a good smile and cuddle were no longer on offer to Leo. He soon learnt that those naughty mistakes should not be repeated.

According to the parent/s, one very important activity that Leo could do to keep himself in very good health almost all his life, is physical exercises. There are, of course, no guarantees of good health for anyone for their whole life. Leo needs to be very healthy throughout the duration of his whole life, as much as possible. Doctors' advice is sought on which exercises Leo can do, at various stages in life, and those physical exercises are done for short durations.

A) It is assumed without scientific knowhow or data that Leo, by doing good physical exercises from childhood and pursuing a very active lifestyle, could help him live a good healthy life up to around age ninety-five. Again, it is assumed without scientific knowledge that by doing those good exercises at a young age, Leo would have developed and strengthened his heart and other organs. Overdoing the exercises is not an option.

B) Leo's parent/s assumed that without proper good physical exercises and an unhealthy, laid-back childhood lifestyle, stuck almost six hours before television and/or listening to music and so on, could develop bad habits. Without good physical exercises, parent/s are worried that health problems could develop around age fifty or sixty years. It is possible that potential heart problems, stroke or diabetes and so on, are more likely to happen to people who do not take part in good physical exercises. Having almost no medical knowledge, the parent/s have chosen the plan A) above for Leo and continue to influence him to follow that plan for life, as best as possible.

Whilst talking further about Leo, good physical exercises become an enjoyable routine, along with some aspects that amount to disciplined routines. They are not fully strict but when

Leo starts learning to do physical exercises, to eat, study, play, nap, do further study, eat, play further and talk with parent/s, before going to sleep for the night, a good routine is established. Having started these routines at an early age, he is not allowed to forget these routines. Let Leo think that this is the normal way for a child to live and grow up. As time passes, at some stage, Leo's parent/s forego his habit of napping during the day. Why not let Leo continue the remainder of the routines as much as possible – and that is what happens. Leo is also given one hour of fun time every day, classed as Leo's activity time. Frankly, that is to allow Leo to do anything that he would like to do, but under the parent/s' supervision and approval. This is helping Leo learn what he would like to do but remain supervised by parent/s. That, and possibly other fun times are rationed, but Leo does enjoy those fun times, as much as possible. With all the other good things that are looked at in this book, one can imagine Leo becoming a more well-educated, healthy and mature individual compared to his peers of a similar age group. Leo is also encouraged to be modest so that he himself or others do not feel that he is special. The parent/s feel that that helps Leo to continue to maintain good friendships with his peer group friends.

A good treat is rationed to maybe once a week. Leo has started to understand that parent/s need to work and earn a living. Leo is beginning to understand that a better, longer time-scale education, can bring better salaries in the future. Leo can't wait to grow up and get a good job and good salary. There is no inclination to be big spender and Leo has started to understand that living well within one's means is the best way to live a good life.

From childhood, Leo's focus is drawn to all the good things that can be done right, by choice. At a young age, Leo is able to understand and accept how best to always do the right things with determination. At the same time, Leo has started understanding clearly what the wrong things are that people can do. These wrong things can be very harmful in the future. Whatever the temptations, Leo is determined not to do bad things which can harm him in the future. The parents have made it their focus for Leo to follow all these details, in life. Leo's friends and peers from the local area are expected to have an average standard of living when they grow up and start working.

During the childhood years, Leo's focus is directed by his parent/s to him achieving double the standard of living when he starts working. The parent/s have gone to great lengths to revise the pep talk every six months, for Leo to focus very hard on studies, look after his health and other things that he needs to do, to have a wealthy, healthy, happy long life compared to his peer group friends. The parent/s have explained to Leo about all the right things to do in life. Leo has understood that developing good habits can enhance about sixty years of life after one finishes studies at the age of about twenty-five. A disciplined routine is put in place where Leo goes to school regularly, returns home and has a snack. He then sits down to finish his homework. He also makes his brief notes about the subjects that he has learnt at school that day. He also reads the subjects that are going to be taught the next day and makes brief notes. At about five-thirty, Leo goes out to play with his friends and comes back about six-thirty to help his parent prepare the evening meal and do cleaning in the house and so on. The family members get together at the dining table about seven-thirty and eat their dinner. Once the dinner is finished, Leo's parent does the dish cleaning and then sits with Leo for at least half an hour going through the homework and Leo's notes of all the studies done on that day.

For Leo, there is no need to behave differently on the surface to draw attention to himself. It is not right to bully any child or get bullied by someone else. So the normal behaviour is projected in day-to-day schooling and so on. Living within one's means is very important in life and Leo has adopted this very well. He almost always wears good clean clothes but does not to wear designer clothes or trainers. He is planning to live his own version of the designer life from age twenty-five to maybe age ninety-five. Even after age twenty-five, Leo has no intention of being a big spender or living a life beyond his means. Up to age twenty-five years are allocated by Leo to 'focus on learning very well' and that is how he is allocating lots of effort to do that.

Most of Leo's time in each week is spent on studies, doing physical exercises, reading, practicing mathematics, talking with parent/s and so on. Leo has a keen desire not only to excel in his normal studies, he is interested in watching specific programmes of history, or to see how things are made and so on. He does like some good comedy programmes and other selected programmes on television. Leo's television watching on average does not exceed a maximum of thirty minutes a day and may be ninety minutes on Saturday and Sunday. Leo finds that he seems to enjoy watching television programmes more because he watches them for short periods only. So in effect, the television programmes become treats for him. Leo has, at the back of his mind, the pep talks his parent/s have had with him. There is a clear choice. When one does many things in a disciplined manner for years and years until, say, age twenty-five and passing a university degree, or degrees, with good grades, it becomes easier to find a good job with excellent salary and prospects. This job may start with twice, may be three times the average salary compared to one of his peer group classmates. So imagine living on two or three times the salary on average during your working life for say thirty, or forty or even fifty years. Some jobs may start on a not very high salary, but have huge prospects of good salary increases and bonus payments. The pep talks by parent/s are arranged about every six months or so, and Leo seems to have started enjoying them. Leo does have some very good times as fun times with the parent/s and feels very close to his parent/s.

Someone, having been 'not good studying' and wasted a lot of time on 'this and that' for most of their studying years, can start with very basic income, hardly able to pay the rent and living expenses. Maybe that someone could struggle financially for years and years.

The above are very difficult talks for a child or youngster to understand and accommodate, one would have thought. But in Leo's case, the above things are not difficult concepts at all. Leo seems to have adopted a mature, clever outlook. He has the habit of understanding some things and would ask if he does not understand anything.

Leo's parent/s found that when Leo was happier, he would sleep better at night and the following day, the teacher at the nursery school would comment that Leo was very well-behaved and very happy, almost all day. The parent/s would even hear Leo on the monitor when he would get up in the morning and say to himself; "I am a good boy; Leo is a good boy." Apparently, the occasional grandmother's visit would remind his parent/s that that was grandmother's habit of praising Leo, being repeated by Leo.

The parents have made it their focus for Leo to follow all these details in life. As the maturity level is improved quite a lot Leo has understood is how safe the world can be for a child like him. On the other hand, Leo understands that the world on occasions can be very cruel in some aspects if some addictions like bad gambling habits or taking drugs are adopted, even in small measures. Leo is far too shrewd to fall for free gambling bets and does not ever want to consider all these because of the chance of addiction at some stage. Leo has understood one fact very clearly. This fact is simply that he can trust his parent/s one hundred percent. There is a lot of trust that is reserved for some other people. But as Leo trusts his parent/s fully, he will discuss any matter with the parent/s and take their advice. Leo reserves his privacy and is very much impressed that even his parent/s respect his privacy. Developing so much shrewdness at such a young age is worthy of praise.

During childhood, Leo is focussing on studying very hard, to achieve a standard of living of up to 100 % and beyond when he grows up and starts working. In addition, Leo would have learnt how to live better and spend less money than some other people. He would start to double his standard of living after very many years after starting work, compared to his friends. That would also include a very large income compared to his initial peer group.

Once Leo has started work, he does not intend taking a back seat and just working. He has shown a keen interest in what he does and also volunteered to take on additional responsibilities related to the job. He did keep a low profile in some aspects but his bosses, the manager and the director, soon realised that Leo had become a dependable employee who could easily handle additional responsibilities. They were especially impressed by the mature approach that Leo was able to adopt, dealing with the company's business. Any important area of need, now or in the future, was realistically documented with desirable solutions, without criticising any individuals. The main aim was to just help the company make progress. Leo was able to do this whilst he kept mixing with all the other members of staff, in a healthy manner. He was also able to show all due respect towards the manager and the director. So for Leo, his first job started really well. With regard to day -o-day working, he would approach his manager on a potential problem that the company was facing, with additional suggestion of how that problem could be solved.

The following four paragraphs can potentially, substantially change some people's lives for the better. The functioning of some companies and organisations could even be improved significantly. These are the 'organised focus one' and 'organised focus two', as discussed in the next two paragraphs.

The organised focus for better living needs to become the centre of attraction, indeed the centre of activity. Focus is on the goal that is very seriously aimed at, and one concentrates all efforts towards that goal. It may not be appropriate to let any issue take over one's life but with a good, consistent approach, it is better to focus on some important issue in life. A very good example is something that happened towards the late nineteen eighties… A financial adviser started working in a bank branch and on the first day, the financial adviser made an appointment to see the bank manager. Before hearing anything that the financial adviser had to say, the bank manager said to the financial adviser, "We are here to serve bank customers and their needs. If someone comes to the bank and asks for financial advice, we will definitely get in touch with you. But we are not here to help the financial adviser to line his own pockets with bonuses." After that brief talk, the bank manager let the financial adviser leave the office. The financial adviser left the office somewhat disappointed. However, the financial adviser was officially allocated by the bank's regional office to work at that bank branch and so that was that. The financial adviser asked the other bank staff to attend a focus meeting. The bank manager was not informed by the financial adviser of this focus meeting. The financial adviser asked the bank staff about any customer who may well have told them of a need to speak to a financial adviser in the previous one year. "None," was the overwhelming reply. The financial adviser asked the customer contact bank staff to raise the subject of any customers who may be needing financial advice. There were some questioning techniques that were discussed. This was to encourage the bank staff to talk to the customers about their needs. Another focus meeting was organised by the financial adviser to meet with the bank staff in two weeks' time. The bank staff started talking to the customers about these things and leads started coming in. Approximately ten months went by after this financial adviser had started working at this bank branch. The bank manager went to the bank's regional office meeting for bank branches and his name was announced as the bank branch that made most substantial progress in sales of financial services. The bank manager was shocked, as he had no idea that the sales were happening to such good extent in his branch. A few days later, the bank manager of this branch asked the financial adviser on the phone, to help him, as the manager's youngster was asking about financial investments and pensions. When the financial adviser volunteered to come down to the bank manager's office downstairs, the bank manager replied that that wouldn't be necessary as the bank manager would himself walk up the stairs to meet the financial adviser. So the big lesson here is how 'focus talks on frequent meetings' can help substantially progress.

Whilst looking at the details above, this book is not qualified to give any financial advice to anyone. Anyone needing help regarding financial services needs to find an appropriate qualified, authorised financial adviser and get advice at their own risk. The author, the publisher, translator or distributor of this book cannot accept any legal or other responsibility.

The so called organised focus two is as follows... One big foundry where tens of people were working had suffered a loss in a particular year. Whilst a new engineer came along, some improvements were made, the director called a staff meeting where available staff could get together. This was the first meeting that was called in the foundry's history. The director explained about the foundry's extent of the loss during the previous year and then went on to talk about the particular technical improvements that were being made. When members of staff were invited to ask questions, it came out clearly that many members of staff were not at all happy about the foundry having made a loss. Most staff members were keen to do something extra so that the loss-making scenario could be stopped and the foundry could start making a profit. One member of staff asked if similar meetings could be held once every month. This was agreed to by the director and the working atmosphere in that foundry improved substantially. The foundry started making some good profits and the morale of the staff improved quite a lot. So the organised focus two for improvement was a success.

Can you imagine what wonders focus meetings can achieve? Why not call them focus meetings, rather than management meetings or monthly control meetings and so on? Success or failure can depend on a number of factors and the companies have to cope with all different consequences at their own risks.

Again, looking at Leo's starting of life story helps bring focus back to the purpose of the story. What a potential wonder it is when even an imaginary baby like Leo, is born. The initial thoughts are about the good health of the baby and the mother. Generally, initial and ongoing care is very good and rightly so. The arrival of the baby, in general is a wonderful occasion for the parent/s grandparent/s relatives and friends. One perhaps does not have time to think and organise long-term plans. There are lots of immediate preparations that one needs to do and that is what gets done. One would keep very busy as looking after the baby is twenty-four hours' work and that takes precedence over anything else. The day-to-day planning and living saturates one's life and there is hardly any time to think about a long-term plan of any sort. May be, one could have done some planning before the baby is born? Earlier planning in some ways can help cope with challenging situations better, perhaps?

The individuals who want to substantially improve their own lives need to learn how to be patient in the first instance. It is very difficult to change a standard of living for the better, very quickly. Parent/s can help a newborn baby in many ways to help grow up until about age twenty-one or twenty-five, with care and an incredible amount of support. It may well be that some parent/s feel that they can care and support the child up to age eighteen only. Both sets of parents are right in their own ways. The care and support until the child- gets to about age twenty-one or twenty-five, is to cover studying for a university degree and other possible studies or work experience as well. That way, along with focus and understanding, the offspring can have very good degree with very good grades and there may be an additional qualification that is acquired too. The young adult still needs an understanding of the culture of needing to work in order to earn a good living.

Let's start with the assumption that living a good life is associated with a lot of happiness and hard work. To consider how an average life is normally lived by an individual is not a difficult place to start. The goal is to improve that by up to 100% or more. The goal is not just monetary but would include better health, a happier family life, and all other aspects of better living. How can the parent/s answer some of the important questions about a very successful life for a child?

Will my baby, child, youngster almost always be healthy?

Will my baby, child, youngster, young adult always be happy?

Will my child, youngster, young adult be very good at studies?

Will my child youngster, young adult almost always listen to me and respect me?

Will my child, youngster, young adult always keep away from bad addictions and bad habits?

Will my child, youngster, young adult always keeps some balance of happiness and self-satisfaction even in difficult times?

Will my child, youngster, young adult, learn to always live within their means and not be a show off?

Will my child, youngster, young adult always dress well without showing off, not get very angry and be able to control their temper, have

good self-respect, but learn not to look down on other people?
Will my child, youngster, young adult always do physical exercise and be healthy most of the time.
Will my child, youngster, young adult work very hard at studies, get a very good qualification, find a good job and get lots of promotions?
Will my child, youngster, young adult, be able to raise a wonderful happy, successful family with a very good partner who they are very happy with?

It will take twenty-five years or so for the child to grow up with the right skills and to start the process of significantly improving their standard of living. Some people finish university degree education around age twenty-one, whilst others may wish to go for post-graduation study or other qualifications and take a few years more. Whatever the difference in approach here, one does need to point out that over the years the parent/s needs to get the youngster to focus on securing a good job and on starting to earn a good living. Life is life-long hard work and not just till age twenty-one or age twenty-five. But all the hard work studying and working need not be just hard work. One needs to enjoy life to some degree whilst studying, and working and doing a job. For those who need to finish studies at age sixteen or about eighteen, there may be a good option of apprenticeships or some good work experience positions available. These can be taken up, as appropriate. One still needs a focus towards good serious working at the appropriate time, and that is the focus that needs to be maintained. The culture of doing minimum work if at all, needs to be replaced by a good work ethic.

Leo's parent/s took care of all the necessary expenses and also ensured that the necessary disciplined was maintained for Leo to finish his education successfully.

Human nature dictates that when something is good, and can be legally adopted/used, then a person would not only let it happen but would embrace it. Any individual reading "Pursue Twice as Good a Life" and adopting many of the ways and means of improving their own life and the lives of their own family members, may consider improving life to whatever extent that may be possible.

Here, why not start from the baby stage and see how one can progress further. As we look at improving the quality of life for an individual's of up to, 100% and beyond, why not consider one miracle solution that can be provided... when a baby is a few months old, let's consider this one aspect of the baby's life – the baby, after a great deal of talking and laughing and so on from the parent, could give a happy smile. Let's focus on that good aspect of the baby… the baby will only smile when the baby is very, very happy. The baby is unlikely to smile when hungry, deprived of good sleep, too hot, too cold, when the nappy needs changing, or they see an angry mum or angry dad. The crux of the matter is that a happy smile is only possible when the baby is very, very happy. Can you focus, concentrate, believe in, realize that a smile, happiness and laughter are the best aspects of a good life – and the baby understands this to a certain degree. So let's concentrate on being happy as a good building block of a good life.

When talking with the young baby, why keep a sad or a serious face? Why not jump up and down with joy and happiness? Why not tell happy jokes that would make everyone in the room smile or laugh? The baby surely would not understand the jokes but would understand the smiles and the laughter. Why not let the baby know how happy you are to see the baby? The baby will hopefully soon start to reciprocate with a smile or even a laugh. Keep the baby happy and smiling for as long as possible, every day. Why not continue that when the baby grows up. Keep the child happy, keep the youngster happy, and do it on an ongoing basis. However, you have to do this without spoiling the child or the youngster's good habits. If you spoil the child or the youngster with frequent treats and allow the child or the youngster, to 'spend money', that could do potentially a lot of damage, in the long run.

The child or the youngster has to learn a lot about the world, how best to live in the world and how best to be happy, almost all the time. Good provision, starting from the baby and toddler stage, is happiness which needs to be encouraged so much so that the baby or toddler experiences happiness up to maybe seventy or eighty percent of the day. Allow maybe twenty percent of the absence of happiness. That is allowed to happen because that could providea good perspective on living a life that is happy most of the time. It is also important to understand the unhappiness and how that affects the life. It is better to be prepared for difficulties in life and learn how to cope with them. It is equally important to learn how to overcome difficulties in life and get on with good living.

This happiness enhancement needs to continue from childhood and through the youngster and adult stage, without in any way giving too many treats or spoiling the child in any way. The parent/s' smiles, laughter and talk with the baby, toddler and then the child needs to continue till the baby, toddler, child starts to feel happiness from inside. The parent/s need to do the best that they can on a daily basis and if it needs to be delayed, one needs to be as practical as possible. If the grandparent comes to visit the baby and the grandparents happily smile or laugh with the baby, would that work? The idea is to have a very happy, baby, toddler or child. In practice the baby and the toddler needs to smile and laugh a lot, and make a good show of it. It is unlikely that the baby will start smiling for no reason or when seeing a stranger. If that happens, it may be the child needs to be taught not to do that. All this is better controlled by the parent/s as much as possible.

It is difficult for parent/s to be happy with the baby if one is not happy oneself for some reasons? Raising a baby is very hard but very rewarding experience. When the baby is crying for any reason, it is probably the parent/s' instincts that will guide the parent what to do. Is it possible to be happy almost all the time, in front of the baby? Why not try your best? Can one pass on that focus, that need to work extra hard to achieve the good things, so that happiness can flourish in one's life? Keeping a good control of living conditions in health, wealth, and above average aspirations and succeeding in bringing up a child well, is a good achievement. A special attempt to get the child to do a lot better generally, hopefully, would be an excellent achievement. too.

How can one help the youngster to grow up without learning to drink too much alcohol, start smoking cigarettes, start bad gambling, start becoming a show off, start spending too much money, and so on? Bad gambling can ruin some people's lives. On the side of caution, one may not want to touch any item that is very addictive or indeed likely to become addictive. None of the bad habits in fact can make someone happy on ongoing basis. The best chance for long-term happiness can be achieved by refusing all the bad habits and proposals from the start. You need to prepare yourself or your child to have that determination to say 'no' to cigarette smoking, heavy alcohol drinking, bad gambling and the use of drugs. This initial courage may help quite a lot in a good life that is planned and lived; the determination to look after your good health and succeed in life, requires a lot of effort and resolve. It is important to do physical exercise, but you need to make sure that you do the right physical exercise. You may need to get help from a doctor or specialist in training for physical exercise, or a physiotherapist. Some people may not wish to follow these paths and that is their own choice.

There are lots of points and matters written here that would require parent/s to plan and think what they want their children to achieve. There are some discussions on possible routes for the parent/s to choose from. In the main, why would one not consider the final results that one would want for their children? The extra effort that the parent/s can put in will certainly help the family. If the discovery journey that parent/s make, which helps them change their own vision that they wish to adopt, then that is all well and good. If, by reading the full book, the parent/s and children can make notes on some final aims that they wish to achieve, then that would be a good start. The crux of the matter is how one can work very hard to achieve those final aims.

And who is asking the excellent parent/s to abandon whatever one/they would have done in any case? Any modifications or alterations that happen would be strictly controlled by the parent/s to their own satisfaction and action.

The parent/s may, on introspection, say that they are good, very good. The parents may feel that they have excellent plans for their children and furthermore, that they are clever, understand the complications of life and how to make progress. Anyone bringing a few potentially new ideas to them, would get a strong scrutiny…. But the final decisions would be theirs, and theirs only. These are like putting the words in the parent/s' minds but the fact is, the final decisions are the parent/s' and parent/s' only. The final responsibilities would also, completely lie with the parents only when one is talking about improving a child's life under the care of their parent/s. When one talks about improving one's own life, the complete responsibility would remain with the individual person only. The author, publisher, translator or distributors cannot accept any legal or other responsibility of any description.

Why not read this book completely and ascertain if any little, big or very big points need to be considered? On the final application, would it make sense to alter whatever is shortlisted to be changed to an individual's needs and desires? The final decisions on the manner of applications would be the duty and privilege of the parent/s and parent/s only.

When it comes to the kind of relationship that the parent/s have with their children, the children need to do some changing and parents need to do some changing, as well. The parents need to ask and discuss what the children would like the parent/s to do or not to do. The children, when asking what parents need to do, can be answered in two different ways. If the parents feel that the child's demands are reasonable and they agree, then the parents can mend their ways. If the parents do not agree to their child's demands or requests, then it may well be that the parents can have discussion with them as to why those changes may not be appropriate. It is also important for the parents to follow the rules of not talking children down or putting them down even jokingly. The babies, toddlers, children, or youngsters should be treated with as much respect as possible. Children and youngsters value their privacy very much and that must always be respected. Also, toddlers, children and youngsters like doing some things like playing with toys, eating the food themselves or writing some points down or so on. If possible, the parent/s may want to let them do that. On most occasions, may be, let them choose their own clothes while shopping.

Some things need to be revised to show some extra importance. Some points are repeated for revision, or the points are emphasized again and again, then the readers' forbearance is highly appreciated.

Improvements in life can happen at almost any time during life. Some improvements are better done earlier in life, than later. But then again, some water may have passed under the bridge... Why not get started from today, if possible? A parenting approach can be revised when it is the right thing to do. And living one's own life happily and healthily is possible for many, perhaps until age ninety-five... why not attempt to help our children do that? Is it appropriate to write down a plan for what the parent/s think should be done, over a period of time? Is it essential to monitor progress and revise some plans, as appropriate?

The best tribute can be paid to some children who do lots of good things that are routine, in their daily lives. They help their parents with chores and in every way possible, as well as have urge to study well and progress as best as possible. They may seem to have a sense of understanding the world better than their peer group and know how to put themselves forward in studies, as much as possible.

All the details in this book are provided in good faith. Some points are repeated for revision, or other points are emphasized again and again to show their importance and so the readers' forbearance is highly appreciated. Individuals and parent/s who use any of the details need to read and adopt details for themselves and their children or relatives at their own risk. They may wish to alter the details to their own version of how any details could be used. The author, publisher, translator or distributor of this book does not accept any legal or other responsibility.

Chapter 3

Parent/s Continuing to Care and Influence Their own Child

How can the parent/s continue to care and influence their own child, for a long time, perhaps for life? In most cases, it is difficult to imagine a better supporter for the child, other than their parent/s. The parent/s do a wonderful job bringing up a child, taking care of every need of the child from baby stage to child, then as a youngster and then as an adult. Even when the young adult starts working and possibly moves out to go and live somewhere else, the parent/s in most cases support the young adult, as much as possible.

It is worth visualizing at what age the child could be allowed to slip away from the parent/s care influence privilege. It is neither advisable, nor practical for the parents to stay twenty-four hours a day for years and years, with the child.

Fortunately, in most cases, one lives in a good safe society where nursery schools, primary school and secondary schools are safe places and the children are able to study, learn how to live in this world and so on. This is done in addition to the lessons that are taught in the classrooms. And the parent/s, having good control and the overall supervisory role, do an excellent job of keeping the child safe. But there are dangers that could possibly subject the child to bad habits or addictions. It may well be within reason for parent/s to have a close enough relationship with the child, where child will hopefully talk with parents.

All the good deeds by the parent/s need to be exercised whether the child is in a state school or in a private school. When the child is very young, it is far preferable for the parent/s to spend a lot of time with the child. Essentially, smiling, talking, playing, doing physical exercises, feeding, nappy changing, and so on, need to continue. Also, helping with school work, homework, planning for the lessons for the following day and reading books are good activities for the parent/s to do to help the child.

Explaining difficulties in life when the child is the right age, are all very important tasks for the parent/s.

It is worthwhile thinking whom abandons whom? Parent/s, one would imagine in some ways do not want the child to drift away. The parent/s in most cases do not want themselves to emotionally move away from the child. Whilst living together, the child, or young adult sometimes starts drifting away from the parent/s' care, influence and privilege. There could be many reasons for this, but it is in the parent/s' and the child's interest that that does not happen. The child goes to nursery school, and then to primary school and so on. The best interests of the child are firstly met by the parent/s. If and when the parent/s care, influence and privilege on the child is being lost slowly, that could cause lots of difficulties for the child. This could be due to outside influences such as social media, television programmes, mobile phones, some others start talking and replacing the parent/s influence, and so on. Again, one does not know what the good parent's influence is being replaced by.

It is wise for the parent/s not to let go of some significant percentage of the full privilege of the carer influence. Allowing the full carer privilege to slip away at the wrong time is not something the parent/s should take lightly at all. Once the child slips away from very good parent/s' carer influence and privilege duties, it is always very difficult to get them back on a full-time basis. Many friends are good at times but there are bound to be variations that could influence the child in some negative way. The child could be somewhat lost to some people's influence that is not helpful in healthy educational activities for example. Friends can be good but a few friends could be a bad influence at times. A lot of time could be spent watching television or listening to music when that time should have been spent studying. The parent/s need to keep good control of the child's spending habits and not let the child become a show-off. Additionally, the child could develop a habit of "not living within one's means" that could, perhaps, affect the child for a long time. The child could learn to get very angry and not be able to control their temper. It is very important that one learns to control one's temper, as not being able to control temper could adversely affect the child life in later life. The child not doing enough physical exercise, not taking education very seriously, looking down on some children/people and not seriously listening to parent/s can become very difficult issues, when the parents are trying to bring the child back to their influence as parent/s and carers. The first solution if one doesn't want to lose one's influence as the child's carer, is to spend an incredible amount of time, constructively with the child. The parent/s need to be the parent/s as well as, kind of, the child's best friend/s, as much as possible. That does not mean the parent/s can allow good discipline that is in the child's interest to slip away.

The day-to-day living, working, need for spare time, housing, bills, mortgage payments and shopping costs and other difficulties that the parent/s face cannot be underestimated. At some stage the child/youngster needs to understand these living difficulties that most people face. But there is a need for good navigation through all the difficulties, as much as possible, for the welfare of the child.

People have varying ability to control spending. In this imaginary person's family, the spending that is required for necessities is estimated at seven hundred out of a thousand pounds' income in a month. So this person is able to spend an additional three hundred pounds every month. One can imagine that that does not generally happen. That possibly means that seven hundred pounds are spent on necessities like rent or mortgage, bills, grocery shopping, travelling and other essential miscellaneous spending. If that person continues to spend almost three hundred pounds additionally every month, they would be living by spending all the income and could be anxious because there is nothing spare left for emergencies. That person may even be spending an additional five hundred pounds, leaving a shortfall of two hundred pounds every month.

So spend, spend, spend … the person in the above paragraph needs to stop. If you are living by spending more than your income, you are very anxious all the time, looking to do overtime, and worrying about how to make ends meet. The main focus on looking after your child has shifted to possible anxiety, a need for extra income and how to make ends meet. Additionally, the child has noticed that the parent is spending too much money, and according to the child's thinking, there is no reason why the child should not do the same. So the child, from a young age gets that spend, spend, spend habit. Again, the parent/s' main focus of looking after the child with care and influence is losing ground in all this. Does the parent need to make changes quickly and shift the focus back on looking after the child, better?

Continuing on such a journey to losing influence on one's child even when the child continues to live with the individual would cost a lot. The child's good welfare and security are at risk when the parent/s are busy trying very hard to earn a living and cover all the living costs while finding the child's carer influence drifting away. It is hugely important to note that that could be accelerated bad effects when the child starts becoming an adult. Cigarette smoking, too much alcohol drinking, bad gambling habits, and use of drugs need to be kept away from the youngster as best as possible. Failing in studies, watching too much television, listening to music a lot of the time, mobile phone distractions and social media somehow take over part of their life, with potentially undesirable consequences.

For the parent/s, and child/youngster both it is very important to maintain a healthy trust, good rapport, good friendship and a good relationship for life and not let either party feel that they have lost the other party, for good. Once that level of relationship is damaged, it takes a lot of hard work to bring it back to a good relationship.

Even when the child is out of sight of the parent/s, the child may go to nursery school or other schools, the parent/s need to conduct themselves as if they are very close to the child almost always. On the other undesirable scale, if and when the child/youngster is lost away from carer influence of the parent/s, the child/youngster is very rarely likely to come back to the parent/s. This can happen even when the child/youngster continues to live with the parent/s.

The parent being completely in control, with the child's agreement, helps the child with a good amount of education that could be in addition to what the child can learn at school. The parent/s, having this excellent cooperation from the youngster, can then help the youngster not to ever consider smoking cigarettes, drink too much alcohol, adopt a bad gambling habit, use drugs, get too angry, spend too much money, be a show off, or talk down to some people, and so on.

It is appropriate that your child, at some stage, could take responsibility for themselves on a full-time basis. It is a wonderful and happy occasion for the parent when the child is clever, educated, healthy and mature enough to safely and happily live independently in this world. At that stage, if the parent is willing to let go of their full carer influence, then there is nothing wrong with that. There may be a good agreement or understanding between parent/s and the child that anytime either feels a reason that they should talk, then talking with either the parent/s or the child, would happen.

Chapter 4

Money – Earn with Good Education

Money is very, very important. There is no question about it. In life, family life, business, owning a house, politics, in a country and many other things, money is very important. Money on most occasions can bring lots of happiness to almost all sensible people. Money has an excellent partner in education. But what about education and happiness? Well, again, good education can bring a lot of happiness to individuals. There may be some good reasons why some people do not get educated. But those who do learn a lot in schools, colleges and universities do almost learn to live with that knowledge of accumulated happiness. In almost all cases, the people who have got lots of education are never unhappy about the education that they have received in their lives. There may be a slight desire that they could have got a bit more education, in some cases.

Private schools are out of bounds for most parents due to high costs. The overall costs of private schools for the duration may add up to huge amounts, which are prohibitive for many parents. Also, if it all goes wrong on the financial front, how would the child and the parent/s feel if future school fees cannot be afforded? To bring the child back to a state school, if that is possible, because school fees cannot be paid may be very difficult and disruptive for the child. In addition, the child needs to feel they are normal or average, not a show-off special person. The child needs to behave showing respect for other people and not looking down on others. So the parent/s may wish to plan the child's life with good flexibilities. Eventually, it is, of course the parent/s' choice.

The parent/s who desperately wish to send their child to a private school need to potentially arrange for a very large sum of money and may well need to drop the idea as it simply may not be possible to afford private schooling costs. All the parent/s at this stage need a very important planning arrangement for the young child. Most parent/s overlook this particular need for very large sums of money if and when this child is old enough to go to study in university. It may not be the parent/s' intention that the child when going to university, find a part-time job to at least partly fund the studying time at the university. Secondly, when hearing about student loans and the size of the debt that one can build up before one has even started earning, it would scare the child so much that they may well drop the idea of going to university. Student loans situations do happen in some countries, which is good, as without those loans being available, some students could not go to university. The idea there is that the students borrow some money and repay the loans when theyget qualifications and start work. They can then make loan repayments where some interest is being paid along with repayments for the loan. Without these facilities of student loans being available, some students would not be able to go to university. It is a lot better if the parent/s save some money every month for child's university education needs. The parent/s need to be financially prepared, mentally prepared and get the child to accept the notion that one would need to go to university and study for years to complete the education.

When the child is going to secondary school, the parent/s need to talk from time to time with the child to plan for the university education. That arranges for the child to be agreeable to go to university for studies.

It is a matter of great importance how Leo would plan his university education. Leo's parent/s want him to make a well-informed choice about university education. The parent/s' guidance on this matter was well thought through as follows... It is perhaps right to believe that a student choosing a career or profession in which one wants to specialize is done after some deep thought by the student. The student may well have taken some advice from parent/s or teachers or fellow student friends and so on. No doubt learning a number of things in school helps in making a choice to a certain degree. It may well be that some students are not quite sure what they wish to do with their lives and a career is initially selected. This selection may be a trial, which hopefully the individual will continue.

When parent/s spoke with Leo about all these matters, the proposal from their perspective was put in this manner. He could have the choice of a few different careers, but it may well be difficult to decide which career he should choose. If a family friend was perhaps a lawyer or doctor or teacher or accountant or banker and so on, maybe he could choose some selected questions that could be asked about those professions. These choices are very important and he was well advised to make a choice that he could hopefully stick with. There may well have been some guidance and explanations that were made available in schools at some point which could be taken advantage of, if that were possible.

It is helpful when Leo can select a career of his choice and stick with that option. Leo wants to strengthen his working towards that choice that he has made and focus is always meant to be towards his chosen career. There is some planning that Leo did, to study the subjects related to the career chosen, that he wants to get qualified in.

Considering the standard of quality of living, how does one calibrate the improvement in living a life in quality terms? Improvement in living life is to be compared to what standard? Let one imagine the average standard of living one's life that is happening at present. Any clever effort at improving the life for the better could hopefully bring some improvements. Parent/s and teachers are going to weigh in, ins and outs, good stuff from the chuff and adding in their experiences. They will hopefully use their ways that they have learnt of turning good for the better. They will also provide an effective filter to help steer the youngsters to better ways and means.

If the life is improved by a hundred percent, that is doubling the standard of living. That would be twice as good a living as would have been achieved, compared to what may have been the case. That will happen not on day one of schooling nor day one of college attendance nor on university attendance nor on day one of starting work. Schooling and further studies would be the extra effort, studying and learning period and start of work would start with modest progress, hopefully on a good salary. The vast improvements made would gradually start with salary increases, clever living, better living and living within one's means. No doubt some folks would start on exceptionally good salaries. In that case, one would hope that modest living may prevail, for long-term happiness. Each person's circumstance could be different and one hopes that one is able to make decisions on good long-term living. Buying a better home to live in, can possibly happen. Finding a fantastic partner and consolidating all the good fortunes for a wonderful life with possibly children can happen.

If the average living standard scale from age twenty-five to age ninety-five is improved by a hundred percent that is phenomenal. All these improvements amount to a better standard of living, financially, health wise, property building, job wise, salary wise, temperament wise, a better relationship with a partner, better upbringing of children, better car and so on.

It is worthwhile thinking in theory, for any person, at whatever stage one is at, to consider one important question. If the person can imagine that compared to the current life I am living, what if my past number of years living had been better by up to a hundred percent? The further question that comes along is about my future life. Is that going to be a hundred percent better?

If I achieve a better life, is that going to be better in terms of more money, better health, an improved relationship that I have with my partner if I am living with a partner, and in terms of the relationship that I have with my children, if I have any?

There is no doubt that some people cleverly work very hard in many ways and are living a very good life. Let more of us join them and be happier. Whilst cleverly trying to improve your child's life, why not give it a go on improving your own life? This is stretching the theoretical imaginary better life further, but when there are chances to learn about improvements in standard of living, why not just give that a consideration? You may be at whatever stage of life that are at but how far can you take your own life improvement? Just look at the positive possibilities for a moment. You can take all the phenomenal credits for your own efforts. This book may have helped, but success or failure can be attributed to a number of factors.

Dealing with needs for excellent education is of such phenomenal importance, one needs to lay some groundwork to understand the implications of getting it right. What if you cannot get it right? So let's explore the scenario of getting it right and what that brings to your life.

A. Excellent education from say age two years old to about twenty-five years is a must for Leo and a great deal of help and encouragement is provided by the parent/s. Leo, starting nursery school at age two, does know a little bit about how to talk and understand. The parent/s decided that Leo is going to get all the encouragement, facilities and even home tuition support that can be organised and well controlled by the parent/s. Over the years, the discussions that parent/s would have with Leo were organised from time to time. The parent/s even made some notes and referred to previous notes, as necessary, to help Leo fully understand and agree with the plan that was being developed by his parent/s. The points crucial for Leo's benefit were to help him understand the needs for note taking on important matters, filing those notes, and referring to them in the future. All these bits and pieces were being done as serious, but fun exercises, in the initial years. At a young age, any time that Leo spent with his parent/s was almost fun for him. Afterwards, the meetings, discussions were kept as serious meetings and the words 'focus development meetings' were first used with Leo. Good discipline helped and encouragement was provided by the parent/s, with talks about the reasons and for the need for good education. In addition to all these, one needs to understand that the parent/s spent a lot of fun time with Leo on outings and some pleasure activities, like visiting the zoo, and so on. These activities were organised by the parent/s, as they felt necessary.

B. The result for Leo is that he is able to earn an above-average salary from age twenty-five to age seventy-five with good career progressions and promotions. At some point, Leo is made aware that people do not need to work up to age seventy-five, but if one is happy working, the salary is good and the individual wants to continue working up to age seventy, seventy-five or eighty, the employer may allow one to do that. Leo is well informed that some people earn salaries and other people can earn double, or triple that salary for many years. Leo is made aware that triple the salary is potentially possible but none of that is guaranteed. But with good studies and good graduation/post-graduation degrees, those high salaries are possible. Speaking with confidence may help! Leo is made to understand all this very well and has bought into the idea that he might as well study very hard to help him earn a very good salary for decades to come.

C. The additional benefit that Leo got from the above is that he is able to find an excellent, well-educated partner with a similar temperament to match and an earning capacity to mirror Leo's career.
D. Life turned out to be excellent for Leo, his partner, and subsequently for their children. The children almost mirrored Leo's and his partner's life.

E. Jensen, another imaginary boy did the opposite in some ways where up to age eighteen, he took poorly to education with too many distractions like television watching for long periods, listening to music taking up a considerable amount of his time, and a lot more time having been spent with friends, social media, on mobile phone calls and this and that to take up almost all his time.
F. Well, this led to low-paying jobs for Jensen from age eighteen which continued until retirement age.
G. Fortunately, Jensen did find a good partner but the earning capacity of the partner was not particularly good because the partner's education was not good. The partner migrated from education at the age of seventeen into low-paid work which almost lasted all their life.
H. Jensen and partner did start a family but the children almost mirrored their own lives in the future.

There is a balance that is needed, whilst the child grows up. The parent/s rightly should always protect the child. Allowing the child to get upset or scared is not an option to be taken lightly. However, wrapping the child in cotton wool, may well allow the child to grow up less prepared to face the real world. For example, the first few days at the nursery school may lead to the child getting very upset and crying on parting from the parent for some hours. The child needs to be nurtured sufficiently to face the world, slowly and carefully.

Someday, the child will need to grow up and 'make it in this world' without parent/s, by their side.

Who is this wonderful baby likely to become? The capabilities of each individual baby are exceptionally varied. They can be most amazing, exceptionally bright or even experiencing unbelievable success. Sometimes, there may be difficulties leading to disappointments. The options on how one can live one's own life are varied. Most people live their lives in the manner that they have learnt to. In most instances planning on better living is desired but not planning well enough during the course of many stages of life does not set one up for improving life for the better.

Well, imagine the following educational scenario which hopefully can encourage some people and their children to fully adopt the great need for excellent education. Can excellent education go along with everything else that children need to learn in earlier years and continue to learn in the future after education is finished?

Education Education Education Education Education
Education Education Education Education
Education Education Education
Education
!!!!!
!!!
!
Potentially, Financially Better, Entire Life?

The above can be called a blessed foundation for an improved education that is advisable for a person to have.

With very good education, at this beginning stage, why not make a list of all the potential phenomenal benefits for almost the entirety of life remaining to you. Yes, the dedication in time, energy and commitment to improving life is important.

There may be many reasons for the problems, failures, disappointments, frustrations, breakdowns, and fall-backs. Perhaps, one can persevere, as a matter of choice?

Whether or not the level of intelligence is important, is a good question. One could go back and forth with this question. A deciding factor for how well educated a youngster can become is important. Generally, the sheer well-disciplined effort of studying hard for years, is important. It is appropriate that a youngster can have little time to enjoy and live a good life. But investment of time and energy in a disciplined manner studying, is crucial. It is very important that homework gets done and extra home studies are done as well. Let's assume that one youngster studies from age two to twenty-five, in classroom settings, for example. A lot of effort and clever intelligence need to be applied to good studying, for those twenty-three years. Let's assume that that individual finds a good job and starts earning a good salary. It is also possible to assume escalating earnings, for fifty years after that. That is twenty-three years' good effort benefiting that individual for fifty years afterwards. It may well be that that person works for only forty years or forty-five years. Retiring at what age would depend on the individual and the employer. If working for fifty years, the number of years of effort, twenty-three, are rewarded by fifty years of less strenuous physical effort. It is assumed that a person with good education can work in an office, like a lawyer for example. Surely, a lawyer will not need to do hard physical labour as a labourer would need to. So having worked very hard studying for twenty-three years would hopefully result in about twice the duration in excellent salary benefits. The need to continue to learn after starting work, generally happens. A better house, car and things will hopefully follow, for the well-educated. A well-educated individual may well have a better chance of getting a well-educated 'partner for life' as well. A very good income for almost all one's life can do wonders for the individual and the family.

Once having convinced a young child at whatever age, say seven, nine, ten and so on, about the link between education and money, the following message needs to be repeated. A child can faff about on social media, mobile phone, be cool, watch television, listen to the music a lot and just keep playing with mates at while they're young and end up with substantially less education and earn less than half an average salary for the rest of their working life. This is compared to studying very, very hard until about twenty-five years of age and then earning on average, double, triple the salary for forty, maybe fifty years after that and being 'super cool', with a super cool partner, and supercool children who will study equally hard and repeat the process. At the age of thirty, it would be good to live in a super cool house, have a super cool car and maybe plan a supercool family, to live well for years. Then the message may need to be repeated every six months or so, until it really gets absorbed. Other activities can be done in moderation.

Chapter 5

Learning to Establish Good Boundaries

A person learned to smoke cigarettes at the age of eighteen for whatever reason, best known to himself. He tried to stop smoking around age twenty-seven. He could not stop smoking cigarettes. He had had one long discussion with a friend who had given him the idea that using nicotine patches was somehow wrong as one would be using nicotine to replace nicotine from cigarette smoking. He refused to go and see his doctor or his pharmacist for advice. It is recommended that one needs to take a doctor's advice. This individual tried very hard to give up smoking, but could not do so.

So the one boundary this person had set up for himself was that he would not use nicotine replacement therapy like nicotine patches to help him give up cigarette smoking. According to him, replacing nicotine with substitute nicotine did not make any sense, as per the discussion he had with his friend. It is noted here that one hopes he is not going to rely on his friend's advice if he becomes very ill. Is it possible he could have stopped smoking cigarettes, if he had taken the doctor's advice and used nicotine patches, if that was appropriate?

Is it possible that in early years of his life, if he had been informed in sufficient detail about the addictive nature of cigarette smoking, he perhaps would have never started smoking cigarettes? What would have happened if he had been informed again and again, about the dangers of cigarette smoking? So the one boundary that this person could have set up for himself at a young age is, 'not to start smoking cigarettes'. If he had done this, he would not have even needed to consider his own boundary of not using nicotine patches to stop cigarette smoking as he would not have even started cigarette smoking.

This person in the main would not cross his own set boundary about not using nicotine patches.

So if a young person can establish some 'good boundaries' in life at a very young age like:

1.) Being fully committed to your studies, over the years, ensures that you can get qualified at graduate level at university or even post-graduation level. You might even do additional studies such as business administration.
2.) Why not establish a good boundary in terms of regular exercise for say twenty minutes a day every day from a young age, to ensure good health, hopefully forever. Different people may select a different time when they want to do exercises. Bear in mind it may be necessary to get a doctor's advice before doing some exercises.
3.) What about a good boundary in terms of not getting too angry and being able to control your temper? You can also talk to a doctor to get some advice on how to control getting angry.
4.) One can establish a good routine regarding consciously taking care of reasonable hygiene needs to keep yourself, your clothes and home clean, as

much as possible. Cleaning your teeth is important for good living. Also, establishing good eating habits that help keep your body, teeth and gums healthy.

5.) Make young toddler learn an initial regime of good discipline, understanding how behave well, not to hit people or other children and not to bite other people or children.

6.) Another good boundary can be set to not do shop lifting and learn to do shopping mainly for necessities only. It is a very good idea not to become a shopaholic or getting into the 'spend, spend, spend' habit.

7.) To aid the commitment to studying, one can establish disciplined routines of doing homework, extra studies and revision times, including preparatory studies for the next day's lessons.

8.) Setting good boundaries to understand all the dangers of addictions like cigarette smoking, alcoholism, bad gambling and drugs. These boundaries need to be set at whatever ages the parent/s consider appropriate.

9.) Setting boundaries that help promote a healthy family life without the need to work long hours doing overtime to pay the mortgage, bills and so on is also important. There is nothing wrong with working overtime for an employer who needs help, some of the time. Other reason for doing overtime might be because the individual enjoys work so much that they are happy to put in overtime. But if the salary is very good, you may not need to do overtime.

10.) Set boundaries to live an organised life. All different aspects that help one to live a clutter-free life can be helpful. All the important documents can be filed properly so that one can refer to them, as may be required. Also get into the habit of destroying papers that are not necessary.

11.) Set and keep very good control of finances to help you to live a worry-free, good life.

You need to adopt a moderate approach on some issues to help you to not becoming obsessive about cleanliness and so on. While exercising moderation is important, some important issues like good studies, cannot be compromised. Becoming obsessive may be evident in a desire to keep control. There is no harm in good control that you need to keep in life, but you don't want to overdo control; the art of moderation may help.

One of the final boundaries that one may wish to set is a determined look at your own current and future life. The notions that you can do well, earn lots of money, control your life in an astonishing manner and so on do not generally just happen to most people. The following details in A), B) and C) point to how imaginary Leo will live his life. Leo's parent/s could facilitate all this. The reader needs to understand that not all the parent/s could afford what Leo's imaginary parent/s could afford. But the message behind the explanations need to be well understood and adopted, as best as possible. Good living, good finances and a happy family life are possible. You need to follow good rules with a great deal of care and discipline. The boundaries suggested to be set are as follows:

A) Assume that Leo is going to live up to ninety-five years of age.

B) Leo has twenty-five years of good support, living expenses are paid in full, and he is given strong responsibilities to behave, study hard and get excellent results, and gain an amazing amount of understanding of life. Leo must reject addictions like smoking cigarettes, drinking too much alcohol, bad gambling and the use of drugs. Also, Leo understands good rules set by his parent/s on disciplined study times, homework, revision of lessons, planning for the next days' lessons and practicing the principles of 'living within one's means'.

C) By devoting good actions for about twenty-five years to B) above, whether his friends and peer group agree or not, Leo is in full charge of the rest of his life for himself and his future family. During his working life, he may earn double or triple the average income every month for many decades, compared to someone who gives in to distractions quite a lot and are not properly educated. Leo can now enjoy a very 'cool' life.

D) Had a youngster messed up on similar activities to B) above and deviated along with other activities like watching too much television, spending too long on mobile phones and social media, not giving enough attention to good education and so on, the results would have been different. The next forty years may well have resulted in near minimum wage earnings, a lot less fun and not even a hint of a 'cool life'. Once retired, he would have not accumulated enough pension to live a comfortable life in retirement as the earnings whilst working would have been too low. There is a possibility of retiring on state pension only. It is not at all cool to default on loan or mortgage payments. It is not at all cool to struggle when shopping for necessities. What sort of life can one give one's family if one is frequently or always short of money?

Chapter 6

Leo's Life

Leo is an imaginary child who wants to grow up with lots of love and support from his parent/s. From an early age, Leo's parent/s have organised the way Leo is going to grow up and live. Leo receives the best advice, getting all the right mix of opportunities and facilities to help him along the way. Leo has learnt and wants to use every trick that his parent/s thought to be good from their perspective, whilst he is growing up. Leo wants to have an almost difficulties-free healthy life, where compromising his integrity is not even a remote option. Leo is determined to work very, very hard in a disciplined manner, following every good trick at his disposal. Fortunately, Leo is very clever and above all other considerations, is determined to work very hard studying whilst growing up. Leo is determined to continue working hard for decades to follow. Yes, a tendency to be even slightly lazy, is not an option.

Whilst growing up, Leo is very much against gambling, and against becoming a gambling addict. Excessive alcohol drinking or smoking cigarettes, even in the future, are not options for Leo. All the details involved in Leo's life are aimed at making his life the best it can be. If someone else wants to look at these options, it is up to the individual or the youngster's parent/s' choice.

Why not consider the options that Leo has chosen? It is possible to plan a good life for the duration of a life time? A small percentage of the population may live an excellent life, throughout their lifespans. Some of them could have got there by some accident, and maybe, having not planned for it. Others have possibly studied hard and worked hard to get to that stage. Could some people try various details provided in this book, adopt some of these ways of doing things after scrutinising them and improve their lives significantly? If Leo is applying all the tricks that are apparently successful, could these tricks work? Leo is going to work very, very hard to achieve success.

The quest to becoming a better person in so many ways is no easy task. One can find good examples of human endurance from history books that would have happened in the past. Some individuals are able to immensely change their lives for the better. How can your life be potentially improved, from whatever stage you are in? Who would not consider an up to hundred percent or better potential improvement in their standard of living? Even a fifty percent improvement is better compared to the current level. How can the life be improved for one's child, grandchild, partner, parent, friend, or anyone else, in the circle of influence?

Wonderful, state of the art, technological and other developments have been happening in the world. The words worth adopting for Leo are integrity, good health, education, happiness, good level of maturity, avoiding being naïve, developing shrewdness, maintaining law-abiding citizen status, and so on. Leo would not excessively spend money. Furthermore, bad habits like gambling, smoking cigarettes, excessive alcohol drinking even in the future are not options to consider. Leo would not lose his temper and uncontrolled anger would not be an option. Leo would live an organised, clutter-free life as much as possible, hoping to live a better life. Leo would not look down on people and always treat people with respect. Readers are asked for forbearance for repeated messages that are important, but then, Leo likes to be reminded all these so that the message gets imprinted in his mind.

Leo is aware that these things cannot be superficially learnt and practices are developed well, to perfection. To adopt them well could take many years. But then, the life needs to be lived well for many, many decades.

In the main, what are the different goals for living a life that Leo can select from?

Goal 1). Leo living his life in an excellent manner.

Goal 2). Leo living his life in a good manner.

Goal 3). Leo living his life in a ‘potluck’ manner.

Goal 4). Leo living his life in a bad manner.

Goal 5). Leo living his life in a very bad manner.

Let’s select the option Goal 2). Leo living own life in a good manner. This is an excellent choice, because keeping it below the first choice, Leo living life in an excellent manner, is done deliberately. As this is a growing up scenario, there is always room for improvement to try and venture into Leo living life in an excellent manner. Leo is allowing for some disappointments that will inevitably come along in life. There are some bigger advantages to selecting Leo living life in a good manner. Leo can unintentionally, slightly fall into other downward Goal positions, without causing some permanent damage.

For Leo, it is a process of learning by trial and error. For Leo, ‘throwing in the towel’ is not an option. Train positive, study positive, do positive, live positive, partner positive, physical exercise positive and devote time to plan and implement positive. Additionally, Leo does almost all the things, being happy from the inside. Somehow being happy, Leo is able to do things better.

There cannot be any desire for Leo to become a ‘bully’. Getting into the habit of ‘bullying people’ is best avoided. If Leo gets bullied at school, the parent/s will need to deal with that, as they see fit.

Is it possible to understand that Leo brought up with right values, is encouraged to make very good progress? Leo’s future family could also do a lot better as well. However, nothing is guaranteed in life. Leo understands that he will need to work very hard for all the good to happen.

What are the most important details that Leo can look into, to achieve living his life in a good manner? This does mean a lot of different narratives and variables, from person to person. Let Leo make choices here, as per the suggestions that are varied.

Leo endeavours to achieve all the good qualities to be chosen from A to U below. This is not to say that B needs to be learnt after A, and so on. It would be incredible for Leo to learn a fair amount from A to U below, say by the time he is age twenty-five years old. Many things in life, as well as in A to U below, need to be continually learnt for the whole of life. The list is not exhaustive. Leo would need to learn almost everything that a normal child/person needs to learn. When Leo finds something additional to learn from A to U below, it then becomes an additional blessing. Any extra learning from the whole of this book that the parent/s find appropriate, would be a fabulous privilege for the child.

A For Leo, one very important aspect of life he has to work out really, really well, is "happiness". It does not mean suddenly smiling in front of any stranger. But Leo has been, is and will continue to be, "happy", almost all his life. That does not mean pretending to be happy. That does mean being "happy" from the inside. Still, Leo is very mature, and understands the spectrum of difficulties in life, the demands of day-to-day living, and managing all aspects of life including finances. Leo is happy and the family and others that can be made happy, would be made happy.

B For Leo, integrity concerning the lines of ownership of principles, honour, virtue, morality, purity, goodness, righteous trustworthiness and incorruptibility are important, throughout his life. Leo is made aware of all these over the years by the parent/s whilst growing up. Leo starts with a clear conscience towards the parent/s, with love and respect that cannot be shaken. People in the world are generally very good except some bad people who are devious and find a person's weakness. Some of these bad people cannot hurt Leo because he would happily talk with parent/s something is offered to him for free, that does not sound right. Whilst growing up, Leo decided to trust his parent/s fully and on important matters, would feel comfortable talking with his parent/s and taking their advice. With a view to be sensible, it is noted that a lot of these good qualities come with hindsight whilst living. But with good parent/s giving good advice on tap, there is no need for Leo to wait for hindsight to teach him. Leo, is in a hurry. Leo decided to learn these at early age and adopt them.

C For Leo, good health is very important in life. Pain, suffering, heart problems, organ failure like kidney failure, diabetes, and other health problems, may well be avoided, as much as possible. Another, very important requirement is to take care of one's teeth. Talking about all these when Leo is just starting out in life may seem out of place. But how else can Leo prepare his own life to be as healthy as possible? Leo does not want to get away with lots of short cuts. Leo's parent/s guided, instructed, cajoled and helped him through all of these. A routine of good physical exercises helps to build a healthy body for the youngster Leo, in addition to the disciplined habit of continuing those physical exercises, for life. Visits to the doctors, hospitals, dentists and other therapists need to be done as necessary. But why not plan life in the manner that helps living a wonderfully healthy life, with a few, if any, necessary visits health professionals? This good healthy life, can last, potentially, all the way through, up to about age ninety-five. Imagine if Leo, being naïve on good health requirements, passes away at age fifty. How many loose ends and devastated family and friends could Leo leave, in that case? That is not going to happen to Leo! Leo is going to look after his health, perhaps up to age ninety-five or even longer. Leo is in receipt of all the vaccinations that are needed.

Cancer is a very big issue for some people, causing anxiety, as well as a number of complications. Why not do as much as possible to avoid some lifestyle issues and habits that significantly enhance the possibilities of one getting cancer, in the first place? You may not totally avoid the chance of getting cancer, but why not reduce the chance of getting cancer substantially? His parent/s told Leo what to do from childhood. From age eight to about eighteen and beyond, Leo would get up at about six am and walk briskly about one mile to the park. Leo would run very fast for about one mile in the park before walking back. It is assumed that in the early years of life, the vigorous physical exercises that is done by an individual, helps to build a very healthy heart and body. When a good quantity of physical exercises is continued on a weekly basis, in general, this helps people to live a very healthy life.

Good dental health is also very important. Special attention for good dental health is highlighted here. When Leo meets anyone, and greets them with a smile, how would it look if two or three teeth are missing? Also, Leo wants his teeth to be white and not stained. One needs to seek help, professional guidance from appropriate sources like dentists, and act as best as possible. Anyone taking on doing new physical exercises are advised to go and seek advice from a doctor, as necessary. At the age of about forty-five, Leo, was told by one of the doctors, “Leo, your blood pressure level is healthy, and quite low for your age. You may live forever.” Leo does not believe the doctor meant forever, forever. But Leo is in no doubt the doctor was very happy!

D Discipline is one of the areas that Leo knows needs to be balanced maturely. What does this mean in practical terms? Perhaps one can learn this better if one looks at discipline for each person at three different levels. (1) Let's say that one person is totally disciplined. That person wakes up at six am, goes for jogging exercise at six thirty, comes home, does studying/reading a newspaper, eats breakfast, goes to work at eight, comes home at six pm watches television for one hour, gets dinner ready, eats, watches television for one hour and goes to sleep at ten pm. The disciplined level applied by this person on scale of one to ten is about ten. (2) Leo has chosen level two as his approach as he wants to be an excellent manager in understanding how to live life. He is capable of solving his own and his peer group's problems. He gets on with other people and is good at finding some excellent solutions for his own home living difficulties. Leo has chosen about seven to eight out of ten as his preferred discipline level. Leo wants to apply a good discipline level almost all his life but with flexibilities that he may apply himself as he would see fit and proper. The details provided here in point two are not likely to be commensurate with the totally undisciplined person in point (3) here. (3) Someone who is totally undisciplined, gets up at whatever time they feel like, goes to work but thinks nothing bad about it and makes excuses for being late, watches television for one to five hours a day and so on. They cook and eat at varying times, sleep for maybe four or six or seven hours a day and do not have any structure to living. They would do what they feel like doing at whatever time of the day or night. The discipline level attributed to the person described here in (3) is at two out of ten could be (3) above.

Leo on the other hand has chosen (2) because he understands the whole concept of a disciplined life from one to ten and puts himself at seven to eight, out of ten. Why a range, one could ask? Leo would say that life is not rigid all the time and he oscillates from discipline level of around seven to eight as per demand and wish at a particular time. You need to get the level of things right to make your whole life very successful. Leo thinks that his selection of discipline level seven to eight out of ten would mirror His happy, healthy, productive, amazing on family values and very successful life.

E Money is the lifelong essential that in many ways, is always needed in significant amounts, helping for good upbringing of Leo. The distractions need to be kept to a minimum, whilst positive help from the parent/s teachers in general, helped Leo to get very good education to graduate/ post graduate levels. The needs for continuing to update on financial matters is important for life. Why not read financial pages of news papers. Something that can help with good finances, for life, is an option that Leo takes keen interest to try to understand. Savings accounts where he would save money would be the starting point for him. He has understood one big control that he has. Unnecessary spending is one thing that Leo has learnt, not to do. Spending money when necessary is fine. But, one thing that is very important for Leo, is that one is always honest with own self, in determining what is necessary and what is not. Extra level of maturity that Leo has gained, does help a lot. Understanding money is a subject on its own and is very important. Proper budget working for one's life and family finances, is needed to work on a continued basis. One may be stretched to understand why one cannot make a list of things that one needs before going for shopping. Why form a habit of forgetting one or two things that one needs and getting two or three things that one does not need? Why keep on piling things that one really did not need to start with and that all because one could not be bothered to make a list, before going for shopping?

F Education, up to around mid-twenty years of age is so very important to Leo; this is one of the areas that is going to take one of the top priorities of his life. For Leo, the ability to earn good salaries commensurate with promotions and excellent enhancements is desirable and necessary for a good life. For Leo, continuing learning in one way or the other throughout life is a good idea. As essential ingredients for helping make life better, a number of skills need to be developed whilst Leo is growing up. This can be followed by looking out for Leo's future family's needs, and planning for that is also happening. Not earning enough and continuing to earn a salary that is not above average, could cause problems. Earnings may be from a very good job after excellent education and training. Earnings may be business related, but the skills to earn good amounts of money are needed. If personal and family expenses exceed some limits, there could be money worries. Leo has done very well in education and has achieved very good university degrees at graduate/post-graduate levels that give him a good starting salary with very good promotion prospects in the future.

G For Leo, developing early maturity is very helpful. Leo is intending to not be naïve about lots of things. It is so important to avoid being naïve, almost throughout life. Compromise on safety is not a wise option, for Leo. Understanding stranger danger in addition to internet stranger danger is a real necessity. Leo understands the need to avoid unwisely putting any details on social media or the internet. How to deal with dangers, in addition to practicing drills like fire drills, is a wise option for Leo. Not succumbing to scams is an art. Leo, at a young age would possibly go to an elder like a grandparent, ask the grandparent to read the paragraph in the newspaper, and let the grandparent explain all these in detail. As well as learning well, Leo has come even closer to the grandparent.

H What does being practical mean? How does being functional and efficient sound? Being practical can be somewhat linked to being organised, filing the necessary papers, destroying the papers that can be destroyed and so on. Which papers could be destroyed is a personal choice for each individual. All the papers that are kept are filed properly by Leo so he can locate the papers easily, when needed. The best option that he chose was to file the necessary papers in an alphabetical order.

That would help to find the required document quickly. Some difficulties come in life. Leo would happily be honest with the parent/s and take their advice. As the years go by, he feels mature enough to make decisions himself. He would happily talk with parent/s when he decides that he wants to talk with them. Learning to live a clutter-free, clean life is an aspect that Leo has happily put in practice.

I Understanding and planning how not to go bankrupt, is an art. Can one become bankrupt as a result of ongoing excessive spending? Leo clearly remembers one of the pep talks by the parent/s on some people nearly going bankrupt, where they just could not stop spending money. The credit card bill for this person was mounting to fifteen thousand pounds and he was just paying the minimum amount. The interest charged by the credit card company was very high, but this person could not get their act together to sort things out. There are some people staying on the edge like that. The parent/s emphasized that Leo should not be one of them. There could be a number of reasons why one can go bankrupt. Not being able to manage incomings and outgoings, a failed business venture, poor health leading to reduced or stopped earnings, burglary (it is important to have adequate insurance which will provide adequate cover on burglary) and some unforeseen circumstances, could result in one going bankrupt. One can plan for rainy days and all sort of unforeseen circumstances. One can have reasonable insurances to help with some sort of disasters. Why even consider paths that could lead to bankruptcy? Anyone who has declared bankruptcy in the past, or a person with very adverse credit rating, perhaps, cannot get a loan or a mortgage for years. Sometimes, if the loan is agreed even if they havea bad credit rating, the interest charged by a lender may be very high. Yes, these things need to be learnt at any age. But learning these details as a youngster, may help Leo for the rest of his life. At what age does a child need to learn these things? That decision needs to be left to the parent/s.

J With a view to developing shrewdness, for Leo, various areas need good education for early teenage years. Shrewdness, kind of being astute, is a good idea and is how some cunning people live; Leo needs to come into contact with them. As Leo grows older, there is a bigger chance of coming into contact with some cunning people and any preparation and readiness to deal with these situations, can help keep him safe.

K Being safe and happy is no small achievement. The current world situation is such that there are close-circuit television cameras and mobile phones can take pictures and videos. These pictures and videos can be used by the police as well as the courts to convict people doing something illegal. Doing something wrong is wrong and Leo would not be doing it. Doing something wrong and going to prison is not an attractive option at all, for anyone! Leo wants to live as a law-abiding citizen.

L Is it worth looking at anger management that needs to be incorporated in Leo's development? If one assumes that Leo had been given everything that he asked for 'til age 8 and if parent/s say no for the first time, could that make him lose his temper? In reality, Leo would have learnt over the years that the parent/s cannot afford everything and also that it is better if parent/s make all these decisions whilst he is young. That is the best way for him to live safely and happily.

M For Leo to consider bad gambling as a 'light potential' issue could be a big folly. Making it easier for one to get hooked on gambling is one of the disasters that Leo would avoid.

N Having rainy day money throughout life so that there are no occasions when Leo has problems paying bills, loans, mortgage and living expenses is important. Earning enough and managing money issues better, as well as spending less money gives Leo the safety and security that he appreciates. Being able to help children or grandchildren a little bit with their needs in the future, is a privilege Leo would like to work towards.

O Leo considers having a good marriage or living together for life preferably with one partner for life is desirable. Leo would work towards this as best as possible. Leo desires the partner's good health and well-being throughout the partner's life. He treats his partner with utmost respect and trust. Why not discuss a reciprocal arrangement with the partner? Marriage partnerships and partnership issues are very complex. Each person has a different way of dealing with these issues. Some divorces do happen and some may not be able to do anything about it. There is no magic solution to partnership issues. If a partner makes mistakes, Leo would discuss the situation as soon as possible. At least one partner has (say) a fifty percent contribution to a good partnership. It is very difficult to change a partner's personality, but you can perhaps change yourself, if necessary. It can only be done with true honesty about yourself. Suffering for a long time due to injustices may not be a good solution and there could be very good reasons why some divorces happen. But Leo would be happier if his partnership can last a lifetime. Leo would try very hard to make a lifelong marriage a success. The complications of divorce/s including extra huge costs of are enormous setbacks. Both parents' and children's heartaches can be avoided if divorce does not happen. But Leo accepts that there are some partnership situations where divorces do happen.

P Leo understands the world, people living in the world, and has a good rapport with people. Leo does not want to ever look down on any person. People need to be treated with respect in the same manner Leo wants to be treated with respect. Looking up to parents, teachers and adults because of respect towards them is fine. One does learn a lot in life when coming into contact with other people. If one looks down on somebody, it is difficult to see how that person can learn anything from the individual being looked down on.

Q Leo does not want to be a show-off. Leo wants to live within his means and not have money worries. Losing one's home for not being able to pay the mortgage payments and have issues due to not being able to pay other loan repayments are not the issues that Leo wants.

R At the appropriate age as an adult, if moderate drinking of alcohol starts at the weekends for example, it may be needed to be kept in check. The amount of alcohol enjoyed is the personal choice of the individual. Excessive drinking of alcohol with the difficulties that that brings is not a choice that Leo wants to have. Going 'cold turkey' in an effort to stop drinking, is not an option that Leo wants to go through. Smoking cigarettes and drinking alcohol causes a number of health problems, including cancer. Even drinking small quantities of alcohol needs to be kept in check. Trying to give up an addiction with or without a doctor's help may be a cold turkey situation. It is recommended that a doctor's advice must be followed, when needed.

S Use of drugs is not even an option for discussion for Leo. Leo is well aware that some people take a chance on trying drugs and soon get addicted. Leo makes sure that he never talks about drugs and will always make sure that he will never take drugs.

T Constantly being busy, having music, television programmes, mobile phones, social media, this and that on all the time, is not a good idea. Living a simple, not lazy life, paying attention to areas that need to be attended to, are good habits to form. You need to think logically and take appropriate actions when you want to seriously do better for yourself. Doing a lot better for your family life is equally as important. As well as understanding all the above, Leo is allocating sufficient time to good cleaning, good cooking, and doing good exercises to keep healthy.

U Leo has developed one exceptional skill. He can adjust to changing circumstances and happenings with ease. There are two sides to such a scenario. Leo does things cleverly to make things happen the way he wants them to happen, so when things happen that way, he is happy and enjoying life. If things happen differently, he would work with the situation preferably without complaining. He would then make changes if he can. Being able to adjust to situations and demands is a clever art! Being able to change the situations and demands as best as possible to one's liking is an art worth having. The one thing Leo has learnt very well is not to blow anything out of proportion. If anything that happens that is not to Leo's liking, he will try to diffuse the situation.

What progress you can make would depend on lots of factors and the desire to get everything right is very good. But in practice, getting only some of the things right may be of help. Living a successful life is very complex and it may well be appropriate to keep some sense of proportion on successes and failures, which happen at individuals' own risk. But all the successes can add to happiness. The author, publishers, translators or distributors of this book do not accept any legal, general, or other liabilities.

Chapter 7

The Most Valuable Possession

The above heading can turn into a very valuable question – the question being, what is one's most valuable possession? That is something that most people would like to know! The simple answer to that could be 'your own self'. Why not look in the mirror? You are your best possession. With the right training, right personality, right circumstances and right abilities, if proper hard work is added, one person can achieve good results.

One big question that can be asked is, 'would you like to see your best possession, yourself, represented by your happy or sad face? It is possible that some people do not like one or two things about their appearance, and they would have liked something slightly different. Someone may not like that their height is four feet six inches and would have been happier if the height was about five feet six inches. When someone suggests that at four feet six inches' height, you could be considered more wonderfully down to earth person, that person suddenly becomes happy with their four feet six inches' height. Why not be kind to yourself about your appearance? A good smile may help!

Imaginary Leo did one thing right, almost always from the start. He kept a happy face because he continued to be happy from the inside. Being happy, he almost always continued to enjoy doing the right things in life. Leo found that adding 'being happy' to all the things that he was doing always worked out very well. Activities like eating, doing physical exercises, studying very hard, finding work, working very hard, and finding an excellent partner, all gave Leo a lot of joy. He was finding better success in general, than the others around him.

Being proud of yourself is very good. Your self-respect is very important. If anyone looks down on a self-respecting person, that self-respecting person will feel very bad. It is also important for a self-respecting person, not to look down on other people. But in life, one needs to be practical, as much as possible. If one is upset about someone's attitude, it may well be better to let it go. Is there any point in holding a grudge? You may wish to reduce contact with or stop dealing with someone who upsets you. Alternatively, you could train yourself to let it go!

Perhaps it is possible to consider yourself as your best possession. Why not look at the mirror, and think, you have a wonderful body, not just a brain, but an amazing brain. No human has built a robot as clever as an 'entire human brain'. Why not be the best friend to yourself. As a well-wisher, why not look after your body better than you may have done in the past. Why not do regular physical exercises to keep your body and brain, healthy? For someone who has not done any physical exercises before, it is necessary to heed a doctor's advice. Why not keep the brain active and healthy, as well? Why not do the good deeds? Yes, keep on doing a good job at work, and be happy about it. Past so-called mistakes from your point of view are done! If possible, try not to repeat those mistakes. Why abuse your body doing things like excessively drinking alcohol? Why not try and reduce alcohol drinking under a doctor's supervision? Cigarette smoking is a bad habit, for the body. Why start cigarette smoking, in the first place? If a cigarette smoker, why not take good advice from a doctor and try and give up cigarette smoking, under supervision of the doctor? Drugs are absolutely devastating for the mind and almost everything else in your life. Do not start taking drugs! If addicted to drugs, see if you can give up drugs under a doctor's supervision. You need to adjust to the good life as much as possible. Looking after your teeth comes somewhere near the top of the list of things to attend to to live a good life. That wonderful smile with excellent white teeth could serve you very well, throughout your life. And you need to remind yourself about the good life, what the good things in life are and even clinch the best life whenever possible. Writing about these big issues, you need to examine if the intentions are good or not.

And how about thinking about your partner? With yourself being the most important person in your life, the partner cannot be far behind or indeed far ahead. Thoughts about treating other people with respect, need to start right at the top by treating your partner with respect. Getting angry too easily needs to be addressed. Why not have an understanding with your partner that an equal amount of good respect needs to be mutual. A very high level of trust, understanding and good treatment needs to be maintained from either side. You may not consider spending too much money to be a bad habit, but doing just that could cause very difficult financial problems. Why not live within your means and not be annoyed when your partner reminds you of just that. Have so much respect for yourself. Have so much respect for your partner. Why not have a very good life?

Apart from yourself or the partner, if you have a partner, let's assume that there is another most valuable possession, that you own… this could be anything, but for this purpose, let's say that that is a painting. Would you let anyone else damage that painting that you like? Would you yourself make a mark on that painting or deface the painting in any way? If you are not going to let anyone else damage that painting and you are determined not to deface that painting, why resort to smoking cigarettes or drinking too much alcohol and damaging yourself. Remember, if you agree, you are your best possession.

Chapter 8

Avoid Addictions

Smoking, too much alcohol drinking, trying to use drugs and some very bad habits like excessive gambling tend to hone in on innocent young lives and colonise them. Once they are well settled, these are very difficult to get rid of. Youngsters, please keep away from them. Once one is addicted to any type of substance or behaviour, it is difficult to give them up. Any new habit, even things like easily getting angry, the habit of spending too much money, generally does not help in real life over the long term.

The issue to understand here is how easily it is possible to let an addiction conquer a person's life. Perhaps the solution is to have very tough entry-point guard to not let an addiction take over a youngster's or a person's life.

People hardly talk about bad addictions. The parents who are not addicted to anything like cigarette smoking, excessive alcohol drinking, excessive gambling and using drugs in some cases, perhaps feel they have no reason to talk to their youngsters about these very bad habits. And what do these bad habits do when they have got people addicted – they cause so many financial and health problems during the victims' lives. Perhaps youngsters who get addicted to cigarette smoking, excessive alcohol drinking and excessive gambling may have not been warned how bad the addictions are from the start!

Parent/s and guardians may wish to consider the experiments that are suggested here when they feel the youngsters are old enough and mature enough to understand the messages behind them and are capable of understanding the true dangers of addictions. The complete responsibility will remain with the parent/s and guardians on how this is done and not with the author, publisher, translator or the distributors.

The youngsters could be asked to draw sketch of Leo, a boy with brilliant white teeth and another sketch of Jensen, another boy with brilliant white teeth. Both Leo and Jensen are assumed to be at school. These can be rough sketches with well-marked brilliant white teeth shown in both the sketches. Alternatively, ready-made sketches or even pictures of non-existent strangers of appropriate age and showing brilliant white teeth could be used for the experiment. It is essential that the points being made are well demonstrated.

Now, the youngsters are asked to draw sketches of Leo and Jensen assuming a number of years have passed. Leo and Jensen have now aged and they are now assumed to be aged fifty. The youngsters are told that Leo never started smoking and his teeth remained very good white teeth because he brushed his teeth very well every day and looked after his teeth over the years. The main part of the reason Leo's teeth remained brilliant white is because he never started smoking cigarettes. So in this sketch, at age fifty, Leo's teeth are shown prominently white and attractive.

Without referring to science, it is assumed that cigarette smoking causes staining of the teeth.

You need to rely on your own judgement if smoking could stain your teeth over a long period. The best person to ask about this is your dentist. Some people may wish to arrange perhaps an overdue dental check-up with a dentist and make an appointment. Whilst the check-up is being done, you may ask the dentist's advice about smoking cigarettes and the long-term potential bad effects on teeth.

For the purpose of imaginary Jensen, at age fifty, his teeth got stained badly over the years. It is thought that this happened because of smoking cigarettes. Jensen, although trying to brush and take care of his teeth, had very stained teeth at age fifty. It is also noted that the staining of imaginary Jensen's teeth had been there for a number of years before age fifty and the teeth staining steadily got worse. Both Leo and Jensen did visit the dentist on occasions but neither had the inclination to go and see the dentist every year. At age fifty, it had taken a huge toll on Jensen's teeth and imaginary Jensen's teeth had become very stained. It is noted that Jensen had tried twice, very seriously, to give up smoking cigarettes, but without success. So much so, Jensen had become aware of how bad his stained teeth were and when speaking, he would try to speak without opening his mouth properly. His self-confidence had reduced and he could not freely talk with people. In addition, imaginary Jensen had become aware of extra risks that he faced with regard to heart disease, possibility also the risk of suffering a stroke or lung cancer, because of him continuing to smoke cigarettes. He also realised that he had paid extra-large tax amounts because cigarettes are very heavily taxed in the United Kingdom. Taxation levels vary in various countries. So Jensen's sketch aged fifty is shown with prominent, yellow, stained teeth.

The above experiments' drawings and aging is done such that they can have a bigger impact and may succeed in some youngsters not starting to smoke cigarettes. The other quick way to pass on the same message may well be showing two sets of just teeth at younger age and two sets of teeth at old age. At old age, one set of teeth could be brilliant white whilst the other set of teeth could show badly they are stained because of smoking cigarettes.

The damage of smoking cigarettes to imaginary Jensen's teeth does not end there. Potentially, imaginary Jensen may need massive dental surgery and some type of dental work may not be suitable for imaginary Jensen. Perhaps, some dentists are reluctant to do some type of dental work for cigarette smokers. It may well be appropriate to ask a dentist's advice. And losing your teeth and replacing them with dentures would reduce the efficiency of eating food, by many tens of percentage points, perhaps. Additionally, extra dental work may well be very painful or uncomfortable. The dental work costs need to be considered as well. The good person to ask about all these is the dentist that you may arrange to meet.

In some ways, the above is a good exercise because the youngsters are asked to use their imagination to picture how people look different when they age from a young age to age fifty. All this cannot be done until permission is given by the parents.

What about the damage that cigarette smoking causes on the inside of the windpipe and the very good lungs that most people have, to start with? The lungs are contaminated and damaged over the years one smokes cigarettes. You cannot scrub your lungs, can you? And starting to smoke, with the intention of giving up cigarette smoking in a week or a year is a big folly. Also, ask the youngster to ask a family friend or a close relative who is older and who smokes cigarettes how difficult it is to give up cigarette smoking, once addicted. Whilst at it, the youngsters may well ask their parents about addictions to excessive gambling and to excessive drinking of alcohol. The parents may not be addicted to anything bad, but would have life experience.

So if some youngsters have ever tried smoking cigarettes, hopefully, they will be persuaded to give up smoking cigarettes, at this early stage. The ones who have not tried to smoke cigarettes, have incentive not to ever even try to smoke cigarettes.

Considering very good care for the teeth is so important, it needs to be well learnt and well implemented, on a daily basis. One could say that your face is one of the best assets for any individual. The face is the face that people look at and respect. Any major shortcomings like missing teeth or stained teeth need to be avoided.

What about other addictions that many people succumb to? Excessive alcohol drinking and excessive bad gambling can harm people and people's lives very badly. Whilst talking about bad addictions, one may well want to include these addictions into the discussions and maybe help some people keep away from these addictions.

All the people of the world need to be respected. Growing up and making a living in this world is not an easy task for many people. There are very many reasons why many people of the world are the way they are. In many ways, many people work very hard to make a living and they deserve a lot of respect. One can hopefully look at a number of future decades and hope many more people can have a lot more enjoyable and healthier lives.

Chapter 9

Potential Likes and Upsets

If you dislike the following: 'upset' 'yourself', please let them pass by.
If you like the following: 'please' 'yourself', please think about adopting them.

The distance between success and failure is sometimes very long. Some people judge other people's lives and declare the results as 'that person's life is a success' and 'that other person's life is a failure'. They may either say this just to themselves or to themselves and to other people. Let's consider a concept where only ten percent is success, and looking at the other extreme, one hundred percent is success? The reality is that some people will possibly say that you have succeeded almost all the time in life, and may even class the life as a ninety percent successful life. The other group of people may say that you have had more than a fair share of failures and may class life as a forty percent successful life. There are no recognised human standards on success rates and failure rates. Most people try very hard in life and find success possibly in the majority of instances, and maybe, are happy with how they have lived their lives.

Keeping a hundred percent control of your own life is very, very difficult. An adult person can decide when to get up, when to eat, what work to do within some boundaries depending on ability, one may be able to find. Choice of partner would have limitations because two people need to agree in orde to form the partnership. Imagine someone trying to control someone else's life hugely or ruthlessly? This must not happen and there could be laws to make that illegal.

We humans are generally very, very clever. We could teach ourselves that living a clean healthy life could be a very happy life, from our perspective and belief. Doing physical exercises say twenty minutes each day could be something that makes us happy. If we don't like it, we could do it for a month or two and teach ourselves to start liking it. We could eat healthily – just needed portions of food and hopefully teach ourselves to like it. When we are young, we could learn seriously to educate ourselves and learn to like studying hard whilst educating ourselves at school, college and university. On many occasions, we could teach ourselves to like doing our job. If very unhappy doing the job, we could perhaps find another job that we could teach ourselves to like. We could teach ourselves to be happier, when we don't spend unnecessary amounts of money. Say we start savings for our huge potential needs for the future and we are happier to see our savings funds go up and up. In future, and being able to buy a bigger house to live in could bring happiness. We could learn to be the one who has not started any of the following: smoking cigarettes, drinking too much alcohol, gambling and using drugs are the very first on the list that you are glad that you have not started.

Doing something seriously wrong to the extent that you can be locked up in prison is something hopefully no human could be happy about. The only parameter there, is how unhappy could you get? Do youwant to explain this in detail to a mature youngster? The answer could be yes and no, or indeed, yes or no. It is the parent/s choice, and rightly so. The reason to explain this to a mature youngster could be that, if, one gets into drugs, it is well known that there are drugs that are very addictive. A drug addict in general can lead to losing possessions and/or losing your house. The drug addict cannot let the addiction go because addiction is not easy to let go. So even the start of drugs could open small doors to prison, possibly in the future. When a drug addict has nothing left, they are known to take the path to burglary, for example. And burglary, like other illegal pursuits, leads to prison. Why go into ruin? In extreme cases, for a mature youngster, one may need to consider training them by sitting them in the bathroom for half an hour to show them what prison life could feel like. Thinking one may need to spend a year in prison is beyond comprehension! These are the sort of training sessions that one cannot perhaps talk about to other people. The final decision and responsibility to have these sorts of trainings, or not, is best decided by the parent/s.

There is a good chance to be good, work hard at studies and at work afterwards and live a happy, comfortable life up to age ninety-five.

The only and the best person who one can change easily, is yourself! This again is not easy for a cigarette smoking or excessive alcohol drinking person. These very bad habits are not at all easy to give up. This cannot be done without a firm resolve. When a youngster is growing up, the parent/s, teachers and peer group help to change the youngster to become a wiser and better person. It is very difficult to change other adult people on matters like, 'how they live', 'how they do things' and 'how they think'. There are occasions when a person thinks that another person, the way he or she conducts themselves is wrong. But it is difficult to change other person. Why not just consider changing yourself to get better, at least in your own opinion?

We humans are resourceful and indeed very clever in the main. We know what is right and what is wrong. Why not correct all the possible happenings in our lives to rights? As much as sible, don't let yourself not fall down in your wn eyes.

The variety generated by differences in the way people live, enhance and prosper is extraordinarily wonderful. It is envisaged that people have learnt variety of different methods, skills, and behaviours on how to live, from their parents, teachers, and their peer groups at various stages. At say, age thirty-seven, one becomes a parent, and that one individual may know how to bring up a child. Why not try your best to bring up the child but, crucially continue to learn from others, about how that can be done, even better?

How does the concept of 'one knows the best about a particular issue' work? You have learnt everything that you know from other people. Why not continue learning some good things, techniques, methods, concepts and a number of other items from others almost always, as well as using your own skills?

A person sometimes takes offense to some advice, saying they do know what's best and do not need advice. Could it be appropriate to bite your tongue especially if someone just gives good advice without evil intent?

Does anyone like being looked down upon, by someone else? If someone looks down on me whilst talking with me, is it possible that I will never be able to look at this person, with respect? Why not learn 'how to give good respect to others' from the English language? In English, anyone of us, almost, never says to other person, 'how is you' (although some people may use that to sound funny). The best way to say that is 'how are you?' Treating people with respect may bring praise and respect in return.

When bringing up a child or indeed children, wouldn't it be better if the parent/s remain 'constant', meaning 'the same'? It is not always possible, and you need to accept that. What if potential separation anxiety could be minimised? Wouldn't it be better for the child or the children, if their home is not moved too many times disrupting continuity for the child or the children? Or would moving a number of times bring a lot more varied experience to life? You have to live in this difficult world with constraints and within your mean. It may also be necessary to move jobs and also move to better residences to enhance the family's living conditions. Will it be possible to keep the child healthy with regular physical exercise and have a consistently disciplined approach to studying well, if one keeps on moving to different locations? It is important that the parent/s think these things through and show some measure of decisiveness.

There is no doubt that people's lives are enormously varied and some people face a number of difficulties in life. Good wishes and praise go to all. Try to keep your cool and avoid getting angry as much as possible.

Any descriptions or details discussed in this book are not the be -ll-and-end-all in any shape or form. The parent/s' vast knowledge and enthusiasm may well help in an exceptional way.

What is a dream life? It is a 'good life' for the duration of life, from birth to ripe old age of about ninety-five, or beyond! All the years of 'good living' constitute a good life. If you can avoid too many 'ups and downs' as much as possible, this could help. It is not worth becoming too rich if it is followed with being too poor. A good life without too much showing off could be worth consideration. Big show-off could lead to too much spending, which is never a good idea. One, of course, needs to dress well, have a good place to live in, drive a good car, have a respectable status in society, and be happy. One feels good about others who are better off, and the best phrase that comes to mind is 'good luck to them'. You should also have humility and be kind, extending good wishes towards those who are not doing so well.

Chapter 10

Partnership

A very calm, constructive and good rapport with child/children needs to be established by the parent/s to develop routine cooperation and trust. Is it better for the child to respect you as a parent, rather than to be scared of you? If you are the best parent authority but also somewhat of a friend to the child, the child needs to have confidence to speak truth when delicate matters like boyfriends/girlfriends arise. The parent may have some thinking to do. Parent/s need to establish some discipline and that is very important. On the other hand, the parent needs to be the child's friend as well. There are no magic answers here, but then again, life is very complex. It may not be possible for some parent/s to develop this kind of partnership with some children.

The potential initial mistakes in love a youngster could make could be very damaging. Some youngsters are targeted because they may have a perceived weakness. Someone taking advantage of them because of a perceived weakness is not a good situation. It is not right if a youngster is targeted and made a partner/friend just because the youngster has a perceived weakness. And where would the relationship end? Future abuse of the partner is possible. Manipulative outreach should be understood and the youngster be made aware of the need to guard against that. You need to think how best to increase the maturity level of the child.

You have to understand that, hopefully, the parent/s are the best judge of the situation of their surroundings and their family. The final decisions and the responsibility for all these decisions that they make will always remain with the parent/s.

To enhance, develop and help a youngster get better results, the parent may well consider forming partnership with the youngster to start the process of helping the youngster do better. There is always a question of the maturity level of a youngster at a young age. The parent/s may consider talking about forming a friendly partnership with the youngster. However, the process may be postponed by the parent/s, if the parent/s feel that the youngster needs to get to a better maturity level before the talks could begin. The main areas of good discipline that the parent/s think appropriate, need to be put in place by the parent/s.

It is not right for parent/s to make fun of the youngster or ridicule the youngster; it is better to treat the youngster with respect. It is perhaps not appropriate to even make jokes about the youngster's shortcomings as their self-confidence could be damaged. If that happens, the decisions in life that youngsters make may be flawed. Even if and when the partnership is arranged between the parent/s and the youngster, there needs to be a clear understanding that the parent/s would have the ability to turn down some proposals put forward by the youngster. There may be a need for discipline that the parent/s need to apply, expecting the youngster to adhere to that discipline, to help the youngster.

It is very important for parent/s to help their youngster to happily agree to the process. When the youngster is mature enough, good reasons for the youngster to form friendly partnership need to be discussed. Some youngsters may well be very pleased that the parent/s are treating the youngster like an adult, to some degree. The reasons why this is being done are very important. The youngster needs to agree with the process and the reasons for engaging in the friendly partnership – it is for the future good of the youngster. There cannot be absolute answers and the situations could be very complex. It is better if final judgements are always made by the parent/s whilst the children are young. When raising a child, two parents need to present a united happy front for the child as much as possible. The situations can get very complex on occasions and there are no magic answers that can be put forward.

It is not advisable to let the youngster have significant amounts of money. A show-off attitude may stray the youngster to the wrong choices. Telling some youngsters, 'don't do it' may well tempt them more to do trials with bad habits. These need to be well managed by the parent/s, so that they don't happen. There are no magic answers for these. The parent/s need to manage these issues in the best ways that they can. It is important for parent/s to understand that these things happen in the society we live in. How best to deal with these issues so that they don't harm your child, is up to the parent/s.

One may be inclined to make a pact with your child. Ask the youngster about three things that the child would wish the parent should not do, and why? The child may say the following:

A. Please do not get angry and start shouting.
B. Please do not put me down (say things like I am not good at studying, and so on) in front of my friends. Please do not do this even jokingly.
C. Please stop smoking.

The parent may say that I will try to remember not to get angry. I will try to remember not to show you down in front of your friends or in front of anyone. I have tried so many times to stop smoking. I am finding it difficult to stop smoking, but I will keep on trying to stop. That is one of the reasons that you should not start smoking cigarettes as it is very, very difficult to give up cigarette smoking. Your health does get badly affected by smoking cigarettes.

What the parent/s may ask the youngster about regarding three things that the parent wants the youngster not to do, or do, can be followed by the parent's choices. It is important that the parent make a note of what they expect their children to do or not to do. It is also important for the parent to remind the youngster about three things that would upset the parent or alternatively, three things that would make the parent, happy. These things can be discussed with the youngster every six months, as reminders.

Chapter 11

Is no Divorce a Possibility?

Is shortage of money likely to cause difficulties when living together? Could that be one of the biggest problems that arises? This happens either when both partners almost run out of money or one of the partners runs out of money. It is possible that there are debts that pile up on both partners or on one of the partners. A person may assume the ownership and say that at first choice, the biggest problem in the person's life is that that person does not have enough money. The individual may even say that the car is not good enough or the house is not big enough and maybe, the wrist watch is not posh enough. All these descriptions may even be real problems. So in real life, a lot of people may probably say that they have not got enough money.

So, when focusing on this problem of not having enough money, drastic steps may help magnificently. If these drastic steps mentioned below are followed by lots of people and these efforts have started some time in the past, they won't find themselves in such a situation. Not everyone's problems can be sorted out. It is probably worthwhile for a lot of people to try some of the techniques stated here. The actions are for the owners' own responsibility and dependent on their own final choices. All the consequences will also belong to the individuals who take these actions. If you want to be very sure that you want to arrange a good master plan to avoid running short of money, what should you do? These may sound like orders but then, if you are serious about certain things in life, you may give yourself such orders and enjoy the fruits or live with the consequences, whatever they may be. Could these be the individual's own commands?

1) You are determined to live within your means.
2) You are going to be very careful about borrowing money and maybe not borrow money if that can be sensibly avoided.
3) You are determined to build up a cash amount in the bank as savings and not

spend the savings unless absolutely necessary. If significant amounts are spent, that would be done as your own decision and as your own responsibility.

4) You are determined not to borrow money from the bank or other institution unless absolutely necessary according to your decision. You realise that it is sometimes easy to borrow money, but very difficult to cope with a significant amount in instalments going out every month whilst paying back a loan that you started.
5) You will keep a very close watch on credit card spending and not pay interest by paying minimum amounts every month. You will arrange for the whole amount outstanding to be taken out of the bank account every month, so that no interest is payable to the credit card account if possible. You will keep a check on these sorts of things ongoing.
6) You understand that every pound spent and every pound paid in interest is money gone and all that adds up. These amounts saved could add up to significant amounts.

7) You will borrow mortgage money responsibly if appropriate, after good advice from a professional adviser at the bank or building society and you will take full responsibility for that.
8) You will take full financial responsibility for your actions and take the bank manager's advice, for example, if necessary.
9) You will continue to responsibly take all the steps to keep your finances in order.

In this book, time and time again, it is written that it is important for you to learn to live within your means. You have to decide if you are going to live with that principle, or not. The second phrase that is used time and time again is "not to be a show-off". You have think about and decide what you are going to do. You may like to and you may find it necessary to wear good clean clothes and clean shoes. Visits to the beautician and hair dressers from time to time may be necessary and spending money on essentials is your correct choice. But then, you should stop impulse purchases and also stop buying expensive designer clothes, shoes, and so on!

The word brainwashing requires a lot of caution. No one likes to be brain-washed and there are extreme cases of untold damage that some brainwashing techniques can result in. Flirting with danger is never a good idea.

You can safely condition yourself to be very, very happy most of the time. Similarly, you can condition yourself to not spend too much money. You can condition yourself to keep a check on your finances. One can condition yourself not to be "a show-off". You cannot go and have leisurely stroll in a clothes shop and end up buying something that you maybe, don't need. There is no use in cheating yourself and pretending that that item that you purchased on impulse, is what you always wanted. You can condition yourself to save significant amounts. Unlike one popular phrase, a lot of savings does not actually burn a hole in your pocket. You may even conditionally learn to pretend to almost not have good savings. And that can, maybe, work whether you have any savings or not.

So overall, can one or both partners agree to take enough steps and agree on good action plans that stop the shortage of money from being one of the reasons for potential future separation or divorce? Come to think of it, that may give both the partners a very happy life, maybe forever. That is the potential or actual partners' own choice.

Being sensible about money and being sensible about lots of things would help many people change their lives for the better. Being able to control your temper and adopting some moderate thinking when that all makes sense is worth detailed thought.

How can two potential partners who wish to live together plan to 'not separate, in future'? It is possible that being separated at some distant date maybe the last thing that they can imagine? Would it make a difference if they are getting married, or plan to live together as live-in partners? For one worthy cause, to look at reducing the chance of separation, you can design an exercise that may help. Both the partners can maybe read two chapters in this book, make notes on up to ten good points from this book and also, up to ten bad points from this book. They can both make notes on those good points and the bad points, and plan to get together to discuss each other's views on each of the points. At the end of this exercise, they may well have understood each other a lot better. After that, these two potential partners have a choice to continue the plan to live together with a lot more confidence. Alternatively, they may decide to part their ways amicably, depending on how each one feels. If needed, surely, they can discuss their plans for the future. It is possible that the two potential live-in partners may have known each other very well before this exercise was conducted by them. One or both of the partners may talk about not doing the above proposed exercise, or that maybe there is nothing wrong with the decision that they make. There are no guarantees on any outcome or hurt or divorce. The author, the publisher, the translator or distributor of this book cannot be held responsible for any legal or other reasons.

Would doing the above exercise give two potential live-in partners or two people getting married a lot more confidence? Only they can answer that question. This can reduce the potential hurt that each partner would feel if they were to separate at a later date. If they do have children in the future, and were to separate afterwards, children may suffer quite a lot. Again, doing all these exercises may put one or both the partners off the idea of living together.

Think back to a possible event you may have witnessed regarding a job interview which you thought felt normal. If you have done roleplay with a friend on potential questions for a job interview, there is a bigger chance of you getting that job. It is very difficult to say to a potential live-in partner that I wish to interview you. Perhaps you should not even think that way. The above exercise can be looked at as understanding the partner better to form a bond that is lot stronger. Well, exercise explained above may well give you a better idea about the type of person your potential partner is, when you starts analysing the discussions in the exercise, and that can actually help both the partners understand each other better.

Leo plans a life with a potential partner that has hardly any possibility of divorce. That is stretching the practicalities of living a life a bit too far. But is it worth a try? A few things that Leo has done well in his life are getting excellent education qualifications, following a very good, simple, clean and healthy lifestyle, and having no addictions that could be classed as bad addictions. Leo is holding down a good job with a good income and is not a show-off. It would be wrong to say that Leo does not get angry. However, Leo has an amazing ability to control his temper and is known to keep very calm under very trying difficulties and circumstances. Leo is very careful to live within his means and is also aware of future huge expenses such as the need for sufficient money for a deposit on a house and the subsequent need to pay the mortgage every month. He is always careful about keeping rainy-day money for emergency use as well. When living with his parent/s, Leo does his fair share of cleaning dishes, clothes and floors and other chores. Doing running around tasks, doing this and that the parent/s ask him is not a problem for Leo.

Not many young adults plan for their future children's nursery schooling and university education savings. Those two items became clinchers when Leo met a potential partner and explained all this, during the third get-together. He discussed his planning of financial needs for all sorts of events for the future. Amongst the other things that Leo discussed, was how he had already set up separate savings fund so that the future children would be able to go to good nursery schools and further on, to university education. He said that he would prefer his future children should not need to get student loans to pay for a university education. The potential partner thought that Leo would be the person to be with for life as he would be more organised than anyone else.

It is possible that no one plans for a divorce when you are getting married, or planning to live together as a couple. Is it appropriate to discuss potential divorce with a potential partner? That seems far too stretched a proposition. You have met a potential partner and there is a wonderful chemistry between you. Everything is going so well and you wish to talk about a potential divorce? Even the start of this discussion can put a good potential partner off the idea of continuing the partnership.

It may well be that some people will take the time to understand their potential partner. Let the potential partner understand you as well. When you and they are both comfortable, you can start the discussion. Even when you are both comfortable with each other, you may not want to have any conversation on that subject. It is each individual's, and partner's choice. You are of course, the best judge of your circumstances and your partner's potential reaction. If and when you decide to start this discussion at your own risk, the potential responsibility has to remain with the person starting the discussion. The author, the publisher, the distributor or the translator of this book cannot be held legally or any other way responsible.

You can always look at the most common reasons for divorce in general. There is potentially a big risk in discussing this with a partner. Could you say to the partner, perhaps we can look at the most reasons why people get divorced so that that does not happen to us. Divorces can happen in a few years after marriage, or a number of years later than that. So what are the most likely reasons people get divorced? If the list is started, initially, let the partner choose potential reasons why people get divorced.

Too many repeats of the word divorce may be off-putting. But the process is to avoid divorce, hopefully, forever and remain married to the end of your life. There is a slightly different discussion if partners decide not get married but remain together.

You would not worry so much about potential divorce were it not for the devastation that occurs for yourself, the partner, finances, emotional turmoil, and other things in life. When a couple starts a family and children are growing up, is it at all fair to burden children with numerous worries if divorce happens?

What is a twenty percent rule? Let's assume that I am living alone. Let me even say that I am one hundred percent happy and I am happy with my life. Let's imagine that I get married, or start living with someone. Let me stretch my happiness and say that my happiness has gone up by twenty percent. So I am one hundred and twenty percent happy now that I am living with a partner that I like and love. Twenty percent is an imaginary figure that may well be four percent or ten percent or whatever.

Let me discuss all this with my partner. Let me say that I am twenty percent happier now that I have a partner that I like. I can ask my partner about this to see if my partner feels the same way. If the partner says yes, then that is wonderful news. If the partner gives a different answer, perhaps we can discuss my partner's answer and find more happiness.

Now I discuss how if I were to lose my partner, say my partner was to leave me, my happiness would drop by forty percent. That means me being one hundred and twenty percent happy will drop to being just eighty percent happy. So my partner increased my happiness by twenty percent but the situation now would result in a forty percent drop in happiness. Having a loving partner leaving me would have a substantial effect on my happiness. I would not want to lose my partner. I would ask my partner if my partner feels the same way.

What about 'focus – no divorce' thinking that you can develop? This can be considered by all couples who live together.

It is possible that some people can have their own way of doing things? Anyone who does something differently can upset others on occasion. The first thing to think about is the consequences of someone doing something differently. Is that going to cause financial loss? If yes, how, much financial loss? Whilst all this is being thought about, you need to keep as calm as possible. Losing your temper does not help. So if the potential financial loss is small and can be easily accommodated in daily living, it may be best to say nothing. It also depends on your temperament and your partner's temperament. Not getting angry and being determined to not get angry can help. If at all possible, gentle discussion around some issues can happen. It may be possible to agree with a partner that you could go for a walk to calm down if a heated discussion starts to take place. You can then come back to 'focus – no divorce' thinking that may be agreed with the partner in very calm discussion. Focus is a very wonderful word. If you keep focus in mind when you want to make a sale of an item, for example, the chance of you selling that item becomes greater. If you keep your focus on good health and go for physical exercise regularly, then there is a greater chance that good health can continue. So, for normally clever people, if you focus on something, achieving it happens more readily – then can the focus on not getting divorced possibly work? In some situations, just the mention of word divorce can upset someone and it may be appropriate not to mention it. Being more tolerant may help quite a lot in some situations. As may be necessary, it may be appropriate to get a doctor's advice or psychologist's advice.

Let's make a pledge with the partner to remain together and possibly have meetings every month to iron out any annoyances or difficulties. This would be done calmly by both, to increase happiness.

Maybe both partners realise that they are both one hundred and twenty percent happier, in sickness and in health and can continue so until death them do part.

How would the partner feel if I bought a shirt that my partner thought I should not have bought? Well, is there any need for me to spend unnecessary money? It is better if spending money is discussed with your partner before spending it. In any case, when budgets are tight, you should not spend money unless absolutely necessary. Also, spending money unnecessarily could be one of the worst habits you can have. Big spenders often experience very difficult times with money shortages and worries.

What about turning a blind eye to very small insignificant indiscretions? Could insignificant breaches being allowed to go unchallenged lead to bigger wrongdoing? It does depend on your relationship with your partner. Well, there is a lot at stake. If separation happens, there is a lot to lose. Both partners need to think, talk and find solutions.

This pushing of the boundaries in the wrong direction may eventually lead to collapse of the relationship. A break up of a relationship, separation, divorce are the phrases and words with massive negative consequences for the safety and security of a family. And what happens to the future of the children, if any, caught up in the crossfire of two adult partners at war?

So what are the options? Go to a marriage councillor, for example, and work things out? Can the couple agree to counselling? Can they agree to work towards calm rational solutions? Can they afford and be willing to pay for the counselling sessions? The circumstances when divorce is sought between two partners is a matter between those two partners, their health professionals and lawyers. The author, publisher, translator or distributors of this book cannot accept any legal or other responsibility, of any description.

There is always a need to have a good mature friendship with your partner, with some give and take. It is worth salvaging a good relationship for your own, your partner's and your children's security and well-being. You can hope for an excellent life with the family. Human life is very complicated. People seeking to get divorced may have varying reasons for wanting this. Can both partners find some acceptable compromise and not go through divorce? That is their own choice and responsibility. You can, however, wish these people good luck for the future.

Chapter 12

A Helicopter's View of Life

Would it be lot better if an individual is, to some extent in good manner, in control of living own life? The other option is, just be a subordinate to the details, surroundings, circumstances and others controlling the life events. When you are able to plan and live life according to own wishes and make things happen in life that are desirable, the enjoyment of living the life increases. With considerable less planning and work, the life living happens as it happens. Lower standard of living may happen and is more likely to happen, that way. How can you control the good standard of living that is made to happen with lot of hard work and dependent on how you performed during educational years? Good educational achievement in the main will hopefully help you to get a good job and potentially a lot better income. So the important question is, what is important for the reader in their own life? It is important for the reader to find the questions and answers.

It is important to be humble to a certain extent. Picking up confrontations is not a good idea because a lot of time and energy is wasted when confronting someone. Being the mature person without putting someone else down, you can find good solution in life and when dealing with others, both parties can be winners.

During childhood years, you cannot be in full control of life. The parent/s in the main do a wonderful job regarding living matters. Leo, the imaginary child needs to study very hard as well as do physical exercise and start learning seriously how to live a good life. All this needs to continue during his youngster years with the view to being prepared to earn and live potentially without his parent/s' help. The parent/s may help for a long time but then the youngster may want to prove to themselves that they are able to make good in this world. Some children are left to their own devices where they try to find how to live life.

How does an imaginary life in prison sound? What, an imaginary prison life? What does that mean? At a young age, a person is so adventurous, people telling the youngster that the youngster cannot do this or that. It is advisable not to smoke cigarettes or drink alcohol. You should not get into the habit of watching television almost all the time. You should not keep on listening to music all the time. You should not consider bad gambling at all. You should not even consider experimenting with drugs. You should not spend lots of money.

The child needs to have one important thing kind of embedded in their mind that is established for good. The simple fact that the child needs to understand is as follows: Say at the age of twelve, the parent says to the child, “How much have you learnt in last five years?” “Lots,” the child may answer. “How much do you think you are going to learn in the next five years?” “Lots,” the child may answer. The parent can explain that, “After I turned twelve, I spent another forty years living in this world. You can imagine how much ‘extra’ I have learnt about life in this world. I want to help you with all this extra knowledge. I am the best friend, carer, as well as supporter that you are going to get in your lifetime. It is in your interests that you ask me questions and take my advice, discuss things and find a good route to take through your life. When I ask you to behave in a particular way or do particular things, start behaving in that way and do those things that I ask you to do. If you want to talk with me to explain the reasons why you do not want to do that, then discuss that with me."

The above talk can be repeated every year until the parent sees that the message is well understood by the child and that they are making full use of what they have been told, by asking the parent the right questions.

The youngster needs to find this right advice that they are given to be convincing. You should not do this and that sounds like they are going to be deprived of this and that. There is a perceived false picture showing someone out there having a better life than the youngster or the individual. The youngster will be open to the advice when they feels that overall, following the advice is a far better choice. It is difficult for the youngster to see long-term advantages, when their peer group/friends, are allegedly having a great time, say smoking cigarettes. When a time line milestone is drawn, say from age eighteen to age ninety-five, starting cigarette smoking at eighteen would fit them alongside some mates who are smoking cigarettes. If they are trying to giving up smoking cigarettes at age thirty or forty, they would perhaps fail. Failing to stop smoking cigarettes, they become a so-called 'cigarette smoker prisoner'. The cigarette smoker may well be calling themselves a 'cigarette smoking prisoner for life'. At age fifty, the teeth of the cigarette smoker are potentially badly stained from smoking cigarettes and they find it difficult to talk as stained teeth become so visible. All the extra taxes paid for the purchase of cigarettes are not welcome. Badly stained lungs from cigarette smoking could lead to lung cancer. Heart disease is one of the likeliest side effects to cigarette smoking. It is best not to pretend to like cigarette smoking when they try it in the first place. Don't do it is the best advice they can give themselves regarding cigarette smoking.

Five or fifteen years of chasing fun and living a pretend dream life would in many, many cases just end up being a difficult life with bad habits, lasting fifty-sixty years, perhaps. You need to understand that without engaging in these difficult, dangerous, life-time habits, there is a lot of fun that you can have out there.

You did not study properly until age twenty-five, and your earnings diminished every year to perhaps half, or less, on average, for the following sixty years. You formed a habit of watching television and/or listening to music almost all the time, forming another bad habit for life, and sacrificed time for good studies, good planning and attaining good maturity levels. You became a bad gambler, started smoking cigarettes, and a bad alcohol drinking habit also became a regular feature. These decisions could be regretted later. Bad spend, spend, spend or other bad habits, could be in and out of life, they do not disappear in general and affect the living standard of living for life.

The good life habits like no bad habits, excellent studying, good physical exercise routines, some time watching good television, good listening to music for some short time periods, very little use of mobile phone, learning good life tricks and getting used to good living are an excellent choice. Earning lots and lots of money throughout life can hopefully be blessed when you find a good partner and jointly live in good house.

Let's look at the example of a large good company's Chief Executive Officer (CEO). You may wish to become a chief executive officer of a large successful company but the vacancies are perhaps less than one in a few hundred thousand, or less. A good CEO is the person who is responsible for the whole company. The buck stops with this person. The CEO manages the whole company with the members of staff who would make sure that the company progresses well, under the good leadership of the CEO. The CEO would want to hear about the good ideas of the employees, encourage innovation, keep a good check on finances, and control all aspects of the good operation of the company.

Let's look at the true reason for referring to the duties and privileges of a good chief executive officer in a company, who can take the company forward. Why not look at "the duties and privileges of chief executive officer of a home"? The main reason for comparing the two chief executive officers is to understand the concept of taking "full responsibility" for keeping, running and progressing the betterment of either the company or indeed the home.

Saying things like, "You are not good at any one of the following," needs to be avoided. Extra learning may be needed to do each task well. I am good at switching on the washing machine and cleaning the kitchen floor. You make sure that you do not spend too much money and keep good finances of the house under control. You cook and look after children well. You also prepare children for a good life of their own, and maintain good integrity and respectable status. You keep the family safe and ensure that good progress in life for all the family members can continue in the future.

You cannot avoid taking responsibility for what has to be done. The buck stops with the individual that is referred to. You may need to do above all yourself or may be lucky to have a good partner to help you. Firstly, you need to be very, very good and then expect your partner to be good. You can enhance the partner's life say by twenty percent. Your partner can enhance your life by say twenty percent. Good joint partnership can enhance both lives immensely.

And if the household has two good earners, two good money managers, two good children raisers, two good tutors for the children, two physical exercise doers and trainers for the children, two almost good cooks, two good cleaners and two law-abiding citizens, you can imagine the progress being made. It is wonderful when both the partners can work on whatever is needed to be done and make progress.

Saying things like "I am not good at cooking," can easily be changed into, "I am not good at cooking very good food, but I can manage a few days eating cheese on toast, making boiled vegetables, or getting some microwave ready meals!" So the idea is not to be helpless if a partner is absent for a few days. Overall efficiency and levels of competence need to be built so that in all areas of living, you can do some things very well, or just about manage some matters. The things that are crucial, like earning a good salary, managing money very well, behaving well within law, keeping a good reputation and other things that feel very important need to be maintained at preferably a good level. You do need an honest approach at doing everything right as much as possible. You lives, you drive, you cook, you learn to be good with looking after money, and so on. Each person does it to a certain extent, why not sincerely try to do it a lot better?

One other very important aspect that Leo seems to have mastered is to be flexible enough to accommodate changes in circumstances and events. He can adjust to various changes that happen, meaning adopting to what needs to be done rather than demanding that the things must be done his way only.

Leo got married and both the partners were very, very happy. Leo's wife was very, very happy but had slight inclination to be a show-off. At their wedding, they had spent huge amounts of money on clothes, the venue, food and other necessities.

Although Leo's and his wife's parents had helped, they still had spent almost all their savings. They both had no cars. Previously, they had used their parents' cars. The wife wanted to buy a brand new car with a bank loan 'to show off' her happy marriage and the imagined wealth potential that they had. Leo spoke with his wife to say that they were both in a uniquely good situation to a certain extent but had to pay rent from now on, as they were living in rented accommodation. Leo also said that getting a bank loan was easy for them but that would put a huge drain on their resources as the monthly bank loan payments would continue for next five years or so. In addition, all this could delay their purchase of a house as their main home and the continued rent payments would be money being spent that could be diverted to payments of a mortgage. The wife agreed to the details of the whole discussion. Buying the first home was a bigger priority and eventually, that would be a kind of a show-off, as well. After discussion, they both decided that they would continue to use public transport and on odd occasions when they needed a car, they could agree with their parents and borrow a parent's car.

The potential shocks to yourself and to the family members in the future need to be managed. There are two distinct ways that this can be done. The first way, on a particular issue, say poverty, can be looked at. The first question is why look at it at all? Well, life is very good, perhaps now, but things could become bad and you may need to live "in poverty" for some time. Also, it is a good idea to at least learn how some other people live in this world. There are two ways to learn how to live in poverty. The second choice is to live a good life in good circumstances and surroundings but at least make a good attempt to think about some people living in poverty. Understanding the poor people's day-to-day struggles and coping with managing of life on small amounts of income is worth a thought even when you do not have such worries. Preparation for changing circumstances with the best intention of managing and coping with good and bad situations is a good life lesson.

The poverty issue becomes crucial when raising children and it is perhaps better if parent/s can prevent them from from living in poverty. They need to be brought up well to allow them to be educated well and attempt to make a good life for themselves. The situation of the parent/s can be varied and there isn't much that the parent/s can do about it. But talking to the child/children when they are a little older about some people living in poverty is worth parent/s' consideration. That way, the children would understand the world that we live in better. If the children ever are forced to live in poverty, it will come as a less of a shock, perhaps. An individual can deal better with mental health issues that some people get when poverty suddenly comes up in life. Some people may be forced to live in poverty and that need can be tackled better if you are already prepared for it. And that is very difficult to teach children if they are being given a very good life where spend, spend, spend is the general culture. Children need to be taught to live well within their means. If the parent can afford certain things easily, but say to the children that this and that cannot be afforded, then that white lie could be very good training for the children. In addition, attempts need to be made to understand so-called rainy day money and saving for the future.

So what about being a very good home CEO? Your child learning those skills from early age may surprise you. One day, your child could become a CEO of a large company. Meanwhile, why not live twenty percent better life with your brilliant partner who has equally added twenty percent to your good life? Even if these are imaginary good life figures, you can at least try to make them happen.

Babies have all the privileges, like being fed on time, nappies being changed frequently, being comforted when crying, smiling when prompted, kept warm, frequent naps/sleep, looked after twenty-four-seven, being loved, getting the necessary inoculations, doctors' and nurses' advice, getting suitable medicines when required, kept clean, well clothed, given lots of attention to and everything else that parent/s think necessary.

It is appropriate to draw a good distinction between privileges and responsibilities. Is a child/ youngster who gets most things that are asked for, likely to have a great deal of difficulty in life? Is it appropriate for the parent/s to agree to child's every request to get something? If that is the case, what happens when the parent says no for the first time? The first occasions when a child/youngster hears no, the individual is likely to find difficulty, in complying. When you hear yes, yes, yes and yes all the time, is it possible that that you may not like no as an answer? People cannot have everything that they want all the time! Is it not the parent/s responsibility to prepare the child/youngster for good living in the future? It is better to live within your means, throughout life. Getting used to excessive shopping is generally not a good idea. We can have good things in life if we are prepared to work hard for them, but only if they are within our reach. And living a good, well-managed life is always better. If you keep on doing lots of shopping, how can you manage the house where things are put in their right places and retrieved when they are needed?

What could give rise to uncontrollable anger? Even if a little anger happens, you need to see if you can control that anger. Anger may not happen, but the logic says that the youngster used to hearing yes almost all the time may not like to hear no and may become angry. Some people show anger in different ways. Some bottle anger up, others start shouting and complaining. Some lose control of themselves and end up doing something silly. It is very difficult to find good solutions to these sorts of issues but knowing the potential problems is a start. The parents do need to think about solutions and seek advice from professionals, as necessary.

What about a youngster who thinks that they are better than everyone else? If someone thinks they are superior, why would that individual learn anything from someone considered inferior? Logically, one thinks that all the youngsters and people should treat other youngsters and people with good respect. Being good to other youngsters and people in practical manners generally means that they would have respect for you and be prepared to help.

Being happy is amazing. Enjoying a treat is wonderful! Giving a treat is fine but there are some details worth considering. Leo may fare a lot better in life if good treats are limited in frequency and quantity. Good treats all the time cannot be good for Leo in the long term. If parent/s spend money like water in front of a child, the child may not understand the value of money properly. The child needs to understand that money is earned after a lot of hard work and the money, is supposed to be spent wisely. Good control over spending money may well help one throughout life. Why not consider a good treat for a child, say once a week or even once a month? Spoiling a child with lots and lots of goodies almost all the time, can lead a child to believe that they are entitled to all the desired goodies for life. That cannot compliment the need for good work for living and living well within your means.

One of the important points to note is that as much as the parent/s needs to be happy with themselves, Leo needs to learn to be happy with himself as well. When Leo looks in the mirror, he should be happy and proud of himself. This has to be done with humility. Leo needs to learn that it is better to treat other children with respect. That forms the basis for treating people with respect in future years. Here, a repeat reminder of very good teeth and very good smile comes to the fore. Leo needs to learn that taking care of his good teeth is essential so that when he looks in the mirror, that good smile can lift the spirit up.

That does mean eating fewer sweets and taking very good care of his teeth. You also need to seriously ensure that you do not smoke cigarettes. Smoking cigarettes costs a lot of money over the years. In addition, there are many health reasons why one should not smoke cigarettes. To top it all up smoking causes lots of stains on the teeth. You need to consider giving up smoking if you have started or you are addicted. Advice from a doctor may be needed. The best trick is never to start smoking cigarettes in the first place!

It is better for the parent/s not to make fun of Leo either in private or in public. This is essential at whatever age Leo is. Leo needs to be treated with respect. Leo needs to treat parent/s with respect. Leo also needs to learn that all the people in the world need to be treated with respect. You should not look down on anyone else in this world.

In terms of having patience through the difficulties that you can incur in life, one of the good ways to prepare yourself is to perform training, so-called drills, for your own preparedness status. This has to be done seriously, with patience.

With imaginary child Leo, only imagination can set the boundaries. These details are stated without any special knowledge or training. The use of training using a "drill" by anyone else in any variant formation is at their own risk. It is noted that the maturity in a child, youngster, or any person, mainly comes from their own experiences living in this world. But parent/s can discuss scenarios that hopefully help the child learn the ways of the world to a certain extent, from discussion.

Leo is told that a training session is to be performed where some important lessons could be learnt by the family members. Leo is assumed to be taken outside of two houses, to look at them from a distance. Leo is informed that this is a learning exercise that would take maybe about two hours. One house appears better from outside by about 20% compared to the house where Leo and family are living. The other house looks about 20% worse than the house where Leo and family are living.

According to the parent/s' judgement, Leo is young but mature enough to understand the details. There is a discussion between parent/s and Leo about keeping these types of training details confidential. The parent explains to Leo that they are going to view a house from some distance, a house that appears to be about 20% better than their own house. On being asked why by Leo, the parent said that all the details will be discussed later. The parent, then stopped some distance from the house that is better than their house said a prayer loudly, so Leo could hear. The parent said that their family wished the family living in that house well for the future. The parent also said that this house appears to be better than our house by about 20% from a distance, from the outside. The parent said to Leo that firstly, it is better to hold on to something that you have got, like the house that they have got, and they should be grateful because they have a good house. It is explained that there is a mortgage on the house, in general terms. It is further explained to Leo that the house could be sold by the bank if the mortgage is not paid for a long period, say a number of months. If the bank gets them evicted and sells the house, they would be in the street or at the mercy of the council. So, it is necessary to keep living, and keep all expenses under control. At this stage, seeing a worried expression on Leo's face, the parent said that everything is in order, and they are paying the mortgage on time. The discussion is taking place only to increase Leo's knowledge. Big spenders can get into debt and may even lose their house. Looking at the better house from outside, Leo is informed that further progress can be made by his own family, if expenses are kept under good control and the earnings are enhanced by a better job, a promotion or indeed, overtime work. If the financial situation of the family can be improved significantly, they could look forward to buying a better house, and move.

The parent takes Leo to see, a 20% worse house from a distance, compared to their own house from outside. The parent again said the prayer for the family living in that house and wished them well for the future. The lesson for Leo is that the parent has respect for that family although they are not known to Leo or the parent. The simple lesson here is that they should respect others and wish them well. The parent explains that there is a family living there and we need to understand that they have worked hard to get that house for their family. Further discussion can go to you losing your job and the potential difficulties that that could bring. There is a general talk about keeping rainy-day (or rainy-days) money that you could need, aside. The talk can even extend to the need for Leo to study well and get a better job in the future. Once Leo and maybe Leo's partner can get good jobs, they can possibly find a good home for themselves.

So the lessons in this training exercise are firstly to appreciate the house and the life that Leo and the family have got. The second lesson for Leo is to have respect for others, whether they are better off or worse off than themselves. There is a lesson to explain that they, like all other people, have to work for a living and the house and other items for living, need to be paid for, in instalments. There is a discussion about not developing jealousy for people who have better things and to wish them well, at least in your own mind. There is a big lesson of not being a show-off and big spender. Then there is a lesson of understanding how mortgages work and having good respect for money. There is a further lesson about Leo to start 'learning to keep secrets from others, the peer groups', not through some sort of ill will, or because he doesn't trust them, but just because everything does not need to be discussed and revealed to others.

Looking at international countries issues and taking some lessons from this whole book as well as from above three paragraphs, there may be some wonderful solutions that may come to some people's minds. Looking at Leo's and his parent/s lives, there may be some good solutions that may help solve some difficult issues that the governmenets face. So taking a helicopter's view of the whole of this book and of Leo's life and Leo's parent/s lives, there are some good points that could be looked at, in the following;

1) Leo's parent/s have taken care of Leo's young life in a complete manner where they have trained, managed, nurtured and helped educate Leo to a very good standard.
2) After a lot of effort, it is assumed that Leo has done very well all his life and done a lot of good for himself and his family.

3) A very important point to understand is that Leo has shown throughout this book that he has not; harmed, taken advantage of, made difficulties for, hurt, threatened, bullied, pressurised any individual or organisation. Leo has achieved more than double the standard of living compared to his peer group friends.
4) Readers are asked to understand a very important point. When Leo's parent/s are successful in raising Leo to be a very good tax paying model citizen, could their neighbours take the same approach? Further to that, if more of the families in the country can raise model children who are wonderfully well educated and become happy model citizens, is it possible that the country's standing in the world can improve quite a lot?
5) Leo's parent/s in this book, bringing up Leo, have not shown any bad feelings for any individual or organisation and looking particularly at above four paragraphs have taught Leo to wish unknown people well. Leo must also not be jealous of other people who are better off and have

better properties. The few lines here are re-written here so that "wishing others who are better off or worse off, good future becomes a norm for Leo". The parent explains to Leo that they are going to view a house from some distance, a house that appears to be about 20% better than their own house. On being asked why by Leo, the parent said that all the details will be discussed later. The parent, when stopped some distance from the house that is better than their house said a prayer loudly, so Leo could hear. The parent said that their family wished the family living in that house well for the future. The parent also said that this house appears to be better than our house by about 20% from a distance, from the outside. The parent said to Leo that firstly, it is better to hold on to something that you have got, like the house that we have got, and we should be grateful because we have a good house.

6) The parent takes Leo to see, a 20% worse house from a distance, compared to their own house from outside. The parent again

said the prayer for the family living in that house and wished them well for the future. The lesson for Leo is that the parent has respect for that family although they are not known to Leo or the parent. The simple lesson here is that they should respect others and wish them well. The parent explains that there is a family living there and we need to understand that they have worked hard to get that house for their family.

7) The excellent lesson for many people in some countries could be that if they behave somewhat like Leo and Leo's parent/s, those people in those countries can help improve their country people's standards of living substantially and those countries can rise as good countries in this world.
8) Stretching the imagination, it is well understood that people need to work and pay the taxes and the officials need to do their government work for people including helping educate the children and youngsters. If and when some lessons are learnt from Leo's parent/s and

> Leo's life shown in this book, a country may do very good progress improving lives of the citizens and there could be better relations between some countries. The people in such country would need to act like Leo's parents and Leo, as best as possible, if they agree? After these words to help get better relations between countries, you can start looking at what continues to happen to Leo.

Helicopter's view, which can also be called bird's eye view may reasonably tempt Leo to give a lecture to his grandfather. These can be called goodwill lectures that are not patronising. Grandfather would have talks with Leo on mobile phone face time some days just to feel close to each other as an extended family. Leo and grandfather also behaved like friends because some jokes would bring them closer as a family. On Leo stating that the melon that the grandfather had left for Leo was very sweet, the grandfather decided to play fun trick on the face time where grandfather was just moving mobile phone up and down saying that he was jumping up and down. Leo picked up on this and said to the grandfather that just moving mobile phone up and down is not good enough as the grandfather had to do his quota of twenty minutes' vigorous exercises as the doctor had said. I want you to be around in good health till your age 95 years and may be beyond, granddad. You must do your physical exercises.

Well that conversation ended amicably when grandfather said that he would go and do his mandated twenty minutes' exercises and so finished the call, laughing.

Maybe, one cannot forget,

Physical Exercises,
Physical Exercises, Physical Exercises
Physical Exercises, Physical Exercises
Physical Exercises
! ! ! ! ! !
! ! !
! !
!

May be healthy life till age 95 or beyond?

That does bring one to important topic of mobile phones and social media. Leo understands the needs for very important mobile phones and social media and so on. When he is a little more mature, he is going to allocate about half an hour each day on mobile phone and social media. He understands the importance of mobile phones and social media and wants to spend half an hour each day on it. But he does not want to spend any more time on these because his focus is education, education and education!

Any exciting propositions, Leo is very willing and happy to listen and adapt to what parent/s or teachers say about improving life in the future. This is very important because some amongst the youngsters do not want to listen to 'lectures from parent/s on how to improve their lives'. Leo understands and knows that the parent/s have a lot of experience of the world. In some ways, Leo considers the parent/s intellectuals, observant, shrewd, astute, perceptive, practical people, with feet firmly on the ground. Leo knows that the parent/s love him very much and discuss important matters that would be useful in future. The main reasons for their own respect for their parent/s is because they are Leo's parent/s and as parent/s, teachers and grandparent/s normally have more experience of living. These are Leo's best supporters with very good knowledge and experience and can help in many cases.

Referring to the initial baby and toddler discussions where being a happy baby and being a happy toddler is meant to create a happy learning habit, happiness becomes the norm. Further continued importance of being happy in childhood and going on to being a happy youngster needs to be a good reminder. How could 'being happy' be extended to help, if possible various life events? Could someone try to learn, 'how not to get upset' as much as possible? Sadness and becoming upset are phenomena worth learning and understanding so when they come, you are able to cope with them. Everyone gets upset! So to rewrite the question, 'could someone try to learn, how not to get upset too badly'? Good use of your own intelligence may sometimes help if you can put in the effort on continuous basis not to get upset, or not to get upset very badly. So the idea is to get 'upset' as little as possible or on occasions not to get upset at all. When someone talks about some matters that upset you and it is beyond your control, it is better to learn not to get upset.

Being very happy from the inside, having a very logical mind that you have developed, being able to control your temper as much as possible and learning to live with the life that you have developed, is something to be happy about. Could it be that ‘being happy’ that way, you may prevent yourself from becoming unhappy? If being very happy is possible, then that is the way to live!

Chapter 13

Understanding a Variety of Perspectives

We have looked at developing the perspective to help Leo understand that it is better to sacrifice considerable time on studying well, leading to him perhaps becoming a successful doctor, lawyer, dentist, an engineer, or a banker, rather than not studying well. A professional earning a rapidly increasing salary from say fifty thousand pounds a year to start with, will perhaps do a lot better in life overall. Ten years after starting on a salary of fifty thousand pounds, the annual income may reach one hundred thousand pounds. There may well even be some additional amounts in earnings, as bonuses for example. Not everyone will start on fifty thousand pounds' salary and in some cases, the salary may be much lower. Could there be more chances of increases in salary, in the future? Again, without appropriate qualifications, salaries could be much lower.

The alternative income level may well start at say twenty thousand pounds a year if you have not paid proper attention and not gotten any appropriate education or degree. An individual may join a lawyer's firm as a clerk and earn twenty thousand pounds a year while a solicitor with degree could be earning fifty thousand pounds a year. The solicitor would be the boss of the clerk. But, the solicitor here may well have sacrificed a lot in time and effort and then become a solicitor.

The solicitor earning fifty thousand pounds a year at the start may find a partner earning say forty-five to fifty-five thousand pounds a year. So the combined earnings of the solicitor and partner may be around one hundred thousand pounds a year. At these salary levels, even with difficulties, it may be possible for them to find a reasonable size house or a flat and five years on, they could comfortably think about having children, perhaps.

The salaries stated may or may not be achieved. There is no doubt that in general, well-educated people earn a lot more money than the not-so-well-educated folks.

An individual earning twenty thousand pounds a year as a clerk may find a partner who earns say eighteen to twenty-two thousand pounds a year. These figures having been taken at random and just suggest an approximate scale of earnings, just to make a point. There is nothing wrong with being a clerk if you are happy about the appropriate earning potential. If not educated well, you may not have a choice in the situation. So the combined salary income for the two partners may be around forty thousand pounds a year. Is it not a much bigger problem getting a reasonable size mortgage, with these earnings? But then again, some people's earnings may be vastly different to earnings suggested here.

With a good perspective from the early years, you may choose to study and work harder and follow the solicitor's example. The better benefits in that case, may help in many ways.

Someone pointed out an example to me recently.... A young clerk at a solicitor's office was earning about half the salary of the solicitor. The young clerk, as a matter of routine, reported to the solicitor. The solicitor whilst earning twice the salary of the young clerk, also, generally acted like the young clerk's boss. The young clerk considered this perspective. The young clerk could feel that the solicitor, whilst being the boss of the clerk, was not cleverer than the clerk. But the solicitor was the boss. The young clerk talked with his parents and went back to study to become a solicitor. As well as earning more than about twice the previous salary, the young clerk, 'now a solicitor' is also a boss!

What about being carefree at a young age? It is wonderful for a baby/toddler where all 'the care issues' are managed by say, the parent/s? Yes, even at the tender young age, the necessary barriers need to climb in in your thoughts and actions. Whilst standing, it is necessary for the child to balance so as not to fall down. The child is naïve, not aware, that unless you balance yourself, you will hurt yourself by falling down. The child needs to learn lots of things!

One could be naïve in so many ways throughout your life. The importance of naïveté must be examined to the fullest extent. Naïve could mean simple, unaffected, ingenuous, or what?

Could you learn not to be naïve, in as many matters as possible? In today's world, it is so easy to be victim of scams. Being streetwise, perhaps indicates more maturity and shrewdness. It is essential to be shrewd as much as possible. It is also essential not to be naïve, as much as possible. We need to learn these things. We need to help our children learn these things.

Is it possible for Leo and Leo's children to have wonderfully healthy lives? Is it equally important for Leo to have a brilliantly wonderful life with funds that he would reasonably need during his lifetime and be able to leave a good legacy?

Also imagine that you are capable of a good life financially, to carry on living well for years to come. You have been able to earn a good living to provide for the partner in life and children as well, helping the children grow up and get university degrees or equivalent and ensuring they are able to settle well into their own lives. You have comfortably lived a life until today and have been happy with all the health, wealth and progress tasks that were undertaken. The own life's desires and goals are reasonably satisfactorily achieved and appear to be on the way to being achieved in the future as well. How does that happen? Who could do this?

There are no firm guarantees in life, health-wise, or indeed financially, that are feasible or possible!

There is a possibility of some guidance to help you improve your prospects. Your individual judgement on how to achieve success or even failure may prevail. Improving your prospects is all down to yourself and your own ingenuity. Making some good decisions and actions may help. What the good decisions and actions are can only be judged by yourself. The success rate may vary from one individual to the other in a wide spectrum of your own scales for measures. The success or failure may adopt a wide spectrum from zero percent to ninety percent or even one hundred percent. You could be your own judge on the measure of success. There are absolutely no guarantees on any front.

People can make a variety of choices and measure their own degrees of success. Also, what happens in later life? Some may be lucky enough to have children. How could you proceed to help the family life for your partner and children? Leave it to chance and it will all probably turn out well? Look at the mess that some people are maybe in – some people live with health problems and some with a large variety of other issues.

You have a wonderful chance, at a young age, to help your own life, for decades to come, to live a healthy long life. You may also have a chance to learn tricks that would enable you to manage your finances, prudently, for many decades to come.

Chapter 14

Parent/s, Children or Youngsters – Difficulties?

There could well be some instances where parent/s do not actually know what to do. After all, bringing up a child or children is one of the toughest jobs that anyone can do! Being exceptionally strict parent/s may not be a good idea. But situations, circumstances and the family issues could differ. You would need to think calmly and hopefully find good useful solutions.

Uncontrolled anger can do huge damage in some circumstances. It is very important to be able to control anger whenever necessary. General good senses depart when uncontrolled anger takes over. The baby, the child, must not be hurt in any way. If parent/s are not able to control their anger, how can the children, whilst growing up, be expected to control anger? Losing your temper must be avoided, always. It is always a good idea to teach children how not to lose their temper. Maybe counting in your mind from one to ten, to see if you can control the temper, is one way. A doctor's help may be needed. There are some things that children need to be persuaded not to do. It is best if these steps are resorted to calmly and cleverly.

While I was writing this book, there have been many occasions where I have taken the approach of sitting on the fence. I wish to help all the readers of this book from variety of perspectives and the word moderate has been repeated.

However, when it comes to the need for education for the children and youngster, there ought to be as much help as possible, and that can be given. The government covers some costs and for university education, facilities like student loans may be available. The student loans may be repayable after the individual starts working and is able pay back the student loan.

One of the joys of living in this world is the variety of people who surround us. There may be no compromise for serious dangerous criminals, but there has to be some accommodation for most other people in this world.

For parent/s, there is no choice but to bring up babies, toddlers and children safely in this world even though some parent/s face many difficulties in so many different ways. Still, the process does offer a vast array of happiness and enjoyment that amount to a treasure for life for the parent/s.

You need to bear in mind that there is a different kinds of discussions of ideas for different groups of people, and you can sometime give more merit to the first group or the second group. It may well be neither of the groups are wrong but their perspectives differ. You may choose to be moderate and possibly sit on the fence. Sitting on the fence, or being moderate and listening to both groups without upsetting either group of people may be the appropriate course of action. The toughest choice could be faced by parent/s on very rare occasions where two children are very different and one is near to parent/s liking and the other's ideas are not accepted by the parent/s. It may be that the parent/s decide to sit on the fence and try to live moderately, accepting both, as best as possible.

To let go of a child, or a parent, or a partner out of your life, could lead to, say forty percent unhappiness for a long time and potentially for life, as well. The figure stated may be ten percent or thirty percent or a different figure. Nevertheless, you note that there is a considerable loss. But to let go is a very difficult choice that some people may need to make. That is a choice for the individuals to make. The author, the publisher, the translator or the distributor of this book cannot accept any legal, or other responsibility of any description.

The only thing that comes to mind is the possibility of moderately approaching or sitting on the fence, which could have salvaged the situation, without needing to let someone go. There could be variety of issues and matters that you need to take into account and so the only people who need to make these difficult decisions may need to seek a doctors' or other appropriate counsellors' or psychologists' advice, as is appropriate.

You almost always love your own child more than anyone else in the world. The best solution for the child and the parent is to ensure that the art and practice of being 'practical' in most situations is vital. So what does being 'practical' mean in practice?

When the toddler is being naughty, it is worthwhile trying to distract them. The barrier to stop the toddler climbing up the stairs is an important practical step for safety. In very rare cases, if someone is being very difficult, causing all sorts of problems, you may need some help, say from a doctor. It is very important that a qualified person's advice, like a doctor's advice is taken, when necessary. The doctor may refer you to a psychologist to get help. At some stage, some boundaries may need to be established, if appropriate. Child safety and welfare are very important, all the time.

There is no doubt that good knowledge that is given to the child over the years, when wisely used by the child, could potentially largely improve the child's life. In addition, a sense of maturity in living a more appropriate lifestyle in this world, could help the child avoid some potentially huge downturns in the future. Whilst growing up, the children do not always take kindly to phrases like 'do not do that', 'avoid that under any circumstances' and 'that could ruin your life if you do that'. There is a tendency that they may wish to try exactly that whenever someone says 'don't do it'! You have to find some solutions to these things.

Some unscrupulous people can badly influence the youngster and then it becomes difficult to bring the youngster to the good side. Any one very bad habit could affect the youngster's life, in part or in full. Imagine that the youngster at a young age could succumb to many bad habits, where survival becomes very difficult. At what age the parent/s talk with the youngster, is up to the parent/s. Whether the parent wishes to talk to youngster, is also up to the parent/s. All the youngsters are different. All the parents are different as well. The parent/s need to decide if it is appropriate for them to talk with their youngsters. They also need to work out if the age of the youngsters is appropriate when discussions take place.

Good discipline boundaries need to be established. It is, in the main, up to the parent/s to decide, how they do that.

Chapter 15

Family

A group of people that you can call family, may start with parents, two partners, children, grandparents, and grandchildren. When are you happiest? Normally, when you are with the family, in general. Family may have two, three, five or more members. Lots of different types of families living together are generally happy. Not all the families are happy families but you can be optimistic that more of the families are happier, compared to the families that are not happy. Even if the grandparent/s are not living with the family, the bond between these members is strong, in general.

You need to seriously think about two sets of household expenses that would incur if two married couples separate or two live-in partners separate. If there is a dispute between the partners and both the partners are very angry, they may not even seriously think about the financial consequences of the separation. Two sets of rents and two sets of heating bills are perhaps just worth consideration before all the issues are considered. And children, if any, may suffer quite a lot, as well.

The family living together happily is a wonderful enterprise, if everyone is happy and does little bits for the family. Imagine two partners cooking separately every day compared to one partner cooking for the family or maybe taking turns to cook. The theme of this book is to point out that the children need to work very hard for years to make their whole life better. In family, all the members need to work very hard to keep all the family members happy and prosperous.

Is it appropriate to think that in many cases, you are happy living together with the family rather than alone? The security of that family is important to the members living together, as a family. Doing any wrong could disturb the happiness of the family. Say, one member of the family is to leave, for some bad reason, then the whole family suffers. The member leaving may need to leave because divorce happens, for example. Some divorces are inevitable and sometimes it is not even wise to stop a divorce happening. But the people living together happily, in general, is a better and more prosperous life for all concerned. This could help the children to get well trained for their jobs that they may get and they may start their own families at some time in the future. It is not possible to imagine that all families can succeed in good living together. The complications in families can be vastly varied. Money worries may be one of the top reasons why some divorces happen. There could be many different reasons and combinations of some reasons may also be applicable. When two people get married, for example, could both the people work towards better harmony over the long term? At good intervals, both the partners may feel comfortable about looking at some issues like money, the way they spend money, security, earnings, current and future needs, aspirations, worries, happy desires and so on. Could this avoid potential married life issues and could that reduce the chance of a divorce? The same logic applies if there are two partners living together as live-in partners and are not married

Spending too much money is sometimes so easily and continuously done by one or both the partners. What needs to be kept in mind is that money is so very important in life for individuals as well as the partners. Family, family security and the future needs of various descriptions, are so important, and you do need to take the issue of not spending too much money seriously. If someone asks, "How does three initial years of unnecessary spending too much money, when less spending would have been wiser, sound?" What would your answer be? Maybe, ten years follow on of heart ache due to a shortage of money even for necessities may result? Taking out a loan is made easier for many people, but the loans need to be paid back, reducing the available money for necessities.

Living modestly is interesting because you are able to keep better overall control, especially on finances. Surely controlling a partner too much is not wise in most cases because you generally get better results with mutual respect and cooperation. Buying genuine necessities like reasonably good work clothes may not be an issue. Saving as much as possible when starting work for example may help with early purchase of residential property. A good savings account may also help with the purchase of a reliable first car. Buying a brand new car may not be wise as a lot of money is needed and again, the loan taken may be required to be paid for a long time. Losing control of your finances because you spend too much money could end up going round in circles as far as finances are concerned. Buying a new car in early years when starting to work, just to show off, may well backfire! Seven years down the line, you may not even be able to afford a second-hand reliable car, is an option that you would perhaps regret.

Chapter 16

Alert and Aware

Being alert and aware is an everyday necessity. Ask yourself, how upset would you be if your pocket was picked or your purse was taken by a thief? If you were alone in a big city, you would not even have fare to get back to home or to your hotel!

Imaginary Leo went on an imaginary journey in a crowded market in a city well known for incidents of pick pockets. If someone had said that he was a victim of a pick pocket, people would not be surprised. In this city, Leo went out with some friends and relatives to a busy market place. The friends and relatives were busy looking at some merchandise in various shops. Leo noticed that a group of young adults were walking behind not too far from their group, pretending to be looking at some merchandise in some shops but keeping a careful look at what Leo's group was doing. To the best of Leo's knowledge, the group that was following Leo's group were potential pick pockets. Leo decided to give the potential pick pockets a fright. He kept making frequent looks towards that group where the potential pick pockets were – there was no mistaking that Leo was watching them with suspicion. The potential pick pockets scattered and soon went away.

Afterwards, Leo talked with the friends and relatives explaining that the group of potential pick pockets were targeting all of them, to the best of Leo's knowledge. None of the others had noticed what Leo had noticed. They all agreed that they would all keep a little watch to see what is happening around and would try to scare off potential pick pockets, like Leo did.

Being a victim of burglary when travelling in a car is no ordinary matter and Leo's being alert potentially prevented car burglary with lots of expensive goods that were in the car. The dangers of people in the car being burgled cannot be underestimated. You or your family member could lose your life or be maimed, and valuables being taken is part of the danger.

Leo, along with his partner and two children went to a place in a particular country and hired a taxi for a few days. The taxi driver was unknown but generally, it was said that crime in that country was minimal. Of course you had to be alert and streetwise. It was agreed with the taxi driver that the taxi would be on hire for six days and in the end the taxi would be released after the agreed payment was made. Leo was very alert and aware of what was happening. For five days the taxi driver was with the family. On one instance, when the family went sightseeing away from the taxi, the family returned after about three hours. Leo's son, about eight years old, said on return that he could not see his designer sun glasses. He said that he thought that he had left the sunglasses in the taxi. Leo asked the taxi driver if he had seen the sun glasses. He said that he had not. The son was very upset about losing the sunglasses. Leo's wife asked the taxi driver to have a good look around to see if he could find the sunglasses. A few hours later on return from another outing, the taxi driver said that he found the sun glasses in the taxi, after all, and gave it to the son.

The above episode about the sunglasses and in general, the taxi driver's insistence that the taxi should drop the family in another city gave Leo food for thought. The family were intending to go to this other city but Leo had developed suspicion about this taxi driver. Leo privately asked one official at the hotel about travelling by train to the other city, but was told that it would be impossible to get reservations on the train at short notice. Leo and family needed to get to the other city the next day.

Leo was in a dilemma. Train reservation couldn't be made at short notice but Leo realised that the taxi driver could potentially have organised the taxi to be stopped and burgled, and what would happen then? With a young family whose well-being could be put at risk, and with valuables, there could be danger. What could be done? Leo could not accuse the taxi driver of organising the burglary in the taxi. He could not even be certain that a burglary was being organised by the taxi driver. So Leo came up with a plan to protect the family and avoid a potential burglary. The solution he came up with was as follows.

Leo had arranged for the taxi to pick them up at nine am. That morning, Leo and family got up early and gave very short notice to the taxi driver saying that they needed to leave straight away at six am. Leo thought that by doing this, there would not be enough time for the taxi driver to liaise with the burglars and they would not have enough time to meet Leo and family at some point on the journey. The taxi driver protested strongly and insisted that they leave at eight am if not nine am. Leo said that they were going to leave at six am and if the taxi driver would not agree, Leo would ask another taxi to take them. Eventually the taxi driver agreed to leave at six am. The taxi driver's reluctance to leave early almost gave Leo proof that a potential burglary was indeed being planned! Just before leaving at six am, the taxi driver went away and made a phone call talking with someone for a few minutes.

Realising that there was no credible option for the taxi driver, he had agreed to leave with the family at six am. Did Leo prevent a potential burglary? Leo thinks the potential burglary was prevented. Being alert and aware had potentially helped.

Leo had a visit from potential builder/burglar at his home. Leo's neighbours were getting some building work done. That was clear from the building materials piled in the front, as well as a half-filled skip at the neighbour's house. An inventive builder/potential burglar knocked on Leo's door and said that the neighbour had hired him to do some work on the roof and the scaffolding would need to be brought in through the little alleyway between them, causing some disruption to Leo. He apologised for that. He also almost barged into the house, saying that he needed to show Leo something at the back of the house. The inventive builder/potential burglar wanted to come into the house but Leo being shrewd, said no. Leo walked the man away after closing the front door properly as he always carried the front door key in his pocket. Leaving the front door open could invite the man's mate to get into the house to burgle. When they went to the back through the alleyway, the man said he was going to do this and that to the neighbour's roof and could also sort out problems of Leo's roof whilst doing that. He added that the dampness problem on Leo's side wall was visible. Leo said no and said thanks for coming but no thanks. All that man wanted was permission to get onto Leo's roof where he would create lots of problems that never existed and keep on billing Leo for a long time. The man was sent on his way. Later, talking to the neighbour, the neighbour said that he had not hired anyone new to do the roof at that time! So this person that came was a potential burglar/builder and a liar! Leo politely, but firmly declined saying he did not want any work done when any cold caller knocked on his front door.

With regard to your house security, is it not better to have good protection? So why not have closed circuit television (CCTV) outside your home? Why not have a monitor near the front door and somewhere inside, so that if someone does come to the door, you could see who it is and whether you want to open the door or not?

Why not have a CCTV recorder inside the home. Why not get a burglar alarm, fitted? It is appreciated that these things cost a lot of money. If you could afford these, it is worth consideration. It is understood that you need to get reputable companies to get these things fitted and there is always the possibility of some risk that you may need to take into account. It is appreciated that not everyone can afford such expenses. Only the reader here could be the judge of that.

Chapter 17

Understanding Latent Heat and Saving Energy?

Many people waste some heat energy through latent heat, as latent energy is not that well known? This section may just save a very small amount in electricity cost for an individual, and indeed, you are talking about a very small amount. But you can imagine how much less energy would be used worldwide, if more people can understand and get into the habit of using little less electricity. This measure will not affect anyone's life adversely. When you look at a worldwide saving of tiny amounts saved here and there, that will add to a significant amount. In any case, it is nice to know about it. Surely, that will make a difference to climate change debate as well?

The automatic kettle switch-off is a great invention as the water boiling in an automatic kettle generates steam which then triggers the switch-off mechanism and automatically switches the electric kettle off. So there are following steps to understand.

1.) Water boils in the kettle and reaches 100 degrees centigrade.
2.) When the water has boiled in the kettle, if the person switches off the kettle, pours the water in a mug or in tea kettle, the temperature of the water is 100 degrees centigrade.
3.) Latent energy (electricity generated and stored when the water turns into steam) is in the steam which builds up in sufficient quantity to trigger the auto switch-off device in the kettle, switching off the electric kettle. This means that for a few seconds, extra electricity is used to produce the latent heat.
4.) Now when the water is poured in the mug or in the tea kettle, the water is still only one hundred degrees centigrade.
5.) If the individual switches off the kettle's electricity using the kettle's on-off switch manually when water starts boiling, the electricity supply is cut off and above step 3.) does not happen. As the

end product is hot water in the mug or tea kettle, at 100 degrees centigrade, the person is not affected in any way.

6.) The electric kettle's auto switch-off device is a great invention. If a person does not manually switch off the electricity supply (maybe, you forget to switch off), the electric kettle will automatically switch off the electric kettle, because the electric kettle has an auto switch-off.

If a little electricity is saved almost every time water is boiled in an electric kettle using the on-off auto switch, across the world, just imagine how much total electrical energy could be saved, in total! Point A) that will happen if more people switch electric kettle off manually each time the kettle gets boiled. Point B) is, if more people in the world do that, it will help some in the battle against global warming. It is also worth noting that when a person thinks about saving a little energy each time say in the morning when switching the kettle off manually to save little electricity, there may be other little things that that person can do to save a little more energy like switching a light off when it is not needed.

It is a matter of focus and that little bit of focus can make some contribution in reducing global warming.

At this time, with the current global energy cost crisis, as well as climate change crisis, someone bringing this to the front page news to the world should be noted. I am not inventing this. All these details, about latent heat, have been known in this world for a very long time. Let many people read all this and start putting this in practice, if possible.

Can this section in the book, Leo's Focus Towards a Better Life' actually start a debate in some countries in the world and make a small contribution to helping people save some money and reduce the climate crisis, in however small a way?

Chapter 18

Excellent Potential Discovery Related to Teeth?

Living a life over the years is a very complex adventure in some ways and in general, you need to work very hard to make good progress in this world. Most people try to take very good care of their teeth and rightly so. The toll of working hard, long hours and running around doing this and that you need to do in life to keep making progress can be heavy. You may look at your teeth and find that a few teeth are missing and some teeth are badly stained. It is possible that a person discusses getting some dental work done with a dentist to and may also look at the possibility of some dental implants put in, to ensure the excellent job that the teeth do like helping eat food and additionally, to keep that good white teeth smile longer. Not all dentists do dental implants and it is possible to find a more experienced dental surgeon who would happily take on dental implants. The gamut of this subject is beyond the scope of this book, but there is one potential new discovery that I have made that might be useful to potential dental implants patients. Whether to get dental work done or not and whether an individual decides to get dental implants done is wholly at the dental patient's own risk and responsibility. The author, publisher, translator or distributor of this book cannot accept any liability or responsibility, of any description.

One of the important points to note is that getting dental implants done is very expensive. The amount of years of experience that the dental surgeon has acquired in addition to the costs involved may well add up to a considerable total amount.

It is very unusual for a layperson like me to make a new dental implants discovery. My new discovery was when my dental implants placements came out of my jaw bone because of one reason that I will explain here. I followed the instructions given by the dental implants surgeon very carefully. I used all the hygiene instructions fully. Initially I drank milk with a straw the next morning and had soup at lunch time, not disturbing the treated side, as much as possible. After about forty hours after the dental implants placements were put in on one side of my jaw, I ate a liquid, soft caramel dessert on the other side of my jaw. A few hours later my dental implants placements came out. The dental implants placements may have come out due to infection but I do not think so. To the best of my knowledge, because the liquid caramel is such a good lubricant, the dental implants placements came out. When other dental implants placements were put in in the other jaw after few months, I ate cereal with milk after about forty hours, again on the opposite side of the jaw to dental implants placement. Those dental implants placements stayed in very successfully. There were further dental implants placements put in and again they were successful because I had not eaten liquid caramel desert.

The dental implants do work wonderfully well for people like me who need them, when everything goes well. My dental implant work was done by a very competent and experienced dental surgeon. All the precautions recommended by the dental surgeon had been followed.

By avoiding a dessert like liquid caramel dessert after the dental implant placements are put in, there is a bigger chance of dental implants placements staying in place. That is my belief.

Having excellent teeth is very important to me and to most people, as far as I am aware. I wish everyone the best of luck with their dental implants.

Chapter 19

Alcohol Drinking and Potential Prostate Cancer Connection

Can prostate cancer be avoided altogether for some men? If prostate cancer has just started, can it be stopped in its tracks? What are the other implications for other types of cancers?

Some men drinking alcohol in general may wish to read my experience of alcohol drinking and my prostate cancer diagnosis, to work out a potentially good plan for the future.

I do need to say that I am not a doctor or a prostate cancer diagnosis specialist. In short, I hardly know anything about prostate cancers or about adverse effects of alcohol drinking. That confirms that no one should rely on any medical, or alcohol drinking matters that I have written here. I believe excessive alcohol drinking, for very short periods, gave me temporary prostate cancer. Please, do not take any detail in this chapter as scientifically proven.

I was diagnosed with prostate cancer and I believe my detailed account can help some people of the world. This can give some thoughts to professors, surgeons and consultants dealing with prostate cancer, on the things that they can look at. It is a well-known fact that cancers are increasing because of the consumption of alcohol. I drank a little too much alcohol for a very short space of time and my prostate cancer was diagnosed after a biopsy was done. I had stopped drinking alcohol completely before even my prostate cancer was diagnosed. Now, I continue to have MRI scans and blood tests but the prostate cancer seems to have disappeared. Did my prostate cancer disappear because I stopped drinking alcohol completely, at the right time? Now, the experts keep on checking me, but my prostate cancer cannot be found. Only cancer experts can advise on this matter, but some research may help.

Further details regarding the writing of these pages are provided below. I was in Mumbai,

India on holiday, in December 2019. Although I have never been an alcoholic, in my sixties there were occasions when I used to drink alcohol in excess. My wife was worried about my drinking and asked a doctor in Mumbai, India, about doing a scan, to check my liver. The doctor suggested that he do the scan of the liver as well as a scan of my prostate. After the ultrasound scans were done, the doctor gave me the result of the scans in the notes as follows.

LIVER: ***It is normal size and echotexture. Portal and biliary radicals are normal. Two small rounded echogenic nodules noted in right lobe measuring approx. 12 mm & 9 mm likely haemangiomas No other focal lesion on mass is noted. Liver margins are smooth. PV: 10 mm CBD 3 mm. No stones in CBD***
This was followed by a note saying:
IMPRESSION: Liver shows two tiny rounded echogenic nodules in right lobe possibly haemangiomas, but needs follow up scans Moderate prostatic enlargement seen with subtle nodular prominence of median lobe noted.

There is no significant post void residue seen in bladder. Rest of abdominal scan normal

The above details given by the doctor in Mumbai, in December 2019 started the whole process.

It is appropriate, I believe, for me to ask people to look at my prostate cancer details written here as these may potentially be useful to some men or their friends, or relatives. Our professors, surgeons, consultants, doctors and health professionals are also urged to look at all this information.

The details in brief could help you understand the situation better:

1) My excessive alcohol drinking for a short duration led my wife to suggest that I have an ultrasound liver scan in India, whilst on holiday.
2) My liver scan was done in India in December 2019. Some abnormality was shown in the liver scan. The actual results as written by the doctor are stated above.

3) I completely stopped drinking alcohol and returned to the UK.
4) I consulted my general practitioner, who very kindly reassured me the best way that he could. He referred me to a prostate cancer diagnosis consultant. Checks were then done in the United Kingdom.
5) My liver scan was performed in the UK. Some liver abnormality, as shown in the liver scan in India, was not showing at this stage. Liver and prostate scan reports were submitted to the prostate cancer consultant.
6) PSA check (Prostate-Specific Antigen blood test) was done in the UK.
7) A complete check was done for cancer through prostate biopsy and MRI.
8) The prostate cancer diagnosis was confirmed after a biopsy, and a very small area of prostate cancer was found.
9) All the options for prostate cancer treatments were explained, very well, by kind professionals.
10) I considered various options, including robotic surgery to remove the whole prostate, a radiotherapy treatment option,

and a focal team to treat localised prostate cancer option to treat prostate cancer found by the biopsy procedure.

11) I selected the focal team approach to treat localised prostate cancer. I met the consultant who kindly explained the approach and treatment. The consultant suggested that a more appropriate scan be carried out after some time had passed. This is to let the prostate heal from the trauma of the biopsy.

12) My imaginary speculation: Did the liver abnormality spread to the prostate area to become prostate cancer, as prostate cancer was diagnosed by biopsy as stated in point 8)?

13) I continued MRI scans and checks of PSA. The PSA check over a period was found around 6, in a narrow range, but was not exceptionally high, considering my age of around 69 years. It was noted that the new MRI scan did not show any signs of prostate cancer?

14) My question here concerns the fact that my prostate cancer had already started as shown by the biopsy. Did stopping

alcohol drinking completely, stop, reverse and cure my prostate cancer? Was this done by my own body? Did this happen because my prostate cancer was spread in very small area, to start with? Or, could it be possible that I am the luckiest man alive? I say that because during the biopsy, the very small bits that were taken in many spots happened in such a manner that all the prostate cancer bits were removed during biopsy. Looking at my life, I would like to differ. I do know, that I am not the luckiest man on earth!

15) It is noted from 8) above that the initial biopsy samples discovered very small amount of cancer in the prostate. According to 13) above the prostate cancer was not seen on the new MRI scan. PSA levels had been maintained in a narrow range but were not too high.

16) Why and how did this happen to me? Why was it not spotted happening to someone else, over the years? I do not know the true answer, or if there is, a true answer to find. The sequence that helped me: (A) I had the liver and

prostate scans in India. (B) I stopped drinking alcohol, completely. (C) My prostate cancer was diagnosed through biopsy. (D) My prostate cancer could no longer be seen on the MRI scan at some point. (E) My not-too-high PSA levels have remained in a narrow range. (F) My concluding question is, did my prostate cancer disappear? Could this be true or is my prostate cancer still there?

17) Is completely stopping drinking alcohol helpful to some other people, in early stages, to stop prostate cancer developing further? Is there any link at all?

18) Did excessive drinking of alcohol for a very short period, actually give me prostate cancer in the first place?

19) Can some experts do some research and find some answers?

20) It is noted to clarify that I have had no prostate cancer treatment of any kind. I am having annual MRI scan checks, which are not showing any prostate cancer, so far. PSA is checked every six months and is within a narrow range. PSA, recorded around 6, is not too high.

This paragraph is very relevant to the overall understanding and the main reasons for me having made my 'big finding'. I figured out the importance of the points listed above, because I was the only one who went through points one to twenty. There is no doubt – the details of the ultrasound scans in India helped me. Different experts and specialists, all were dealing with one or two of my details at a time, so I got the complete picture (a true picture to the best of my knowledge) and understood the complete sequence of events. The liver scan done in India helped me. The prostate scan done in India helped me. I stopped drinking alcohol and that helped me. All these events, happening in the manner that they did, helped me, as well.

I do not know anything about prostate cancer, or any type of cancer and if anyone follows my example and delays treatment, they would be doing that at their own risk. I recommend that people listen to medical experts' and specialists' advice. I had selected one of the options for treatment, recommended by my medical specialist. No one had told me to stop drinking alcohol. I believe my decision to stop drinking alcohol helped me.

I hope that all the people affected should rely on medical expert opinions and advice and make up their own minds. My example is an example of an ordinary person.

The subject of giving up alcohol drinking, or reducing alcohol drinking is very complex as far as my little knowledge on the subject goes. Anyone planning to give up drinking alcohol or reducing their alcohol intake needs to take their doctors', medics' and/or specialists' advice. Anyone wishing to find out about PSA levels, or about prostate cancer needs to take a doctor's or prostate cancer consultant's advice. The author cannot accept any responsibility of any kind.

My PSA blood test done by my Doctor was found to be around six. This is not considered too high for my age range, to the best of my knowledge. This is a complex area of medicine and people should heed the advice of their doctor or prostate cancer consultant. A PSA test is a test of Prostate-Specific Antigens in the blood.

What is shown below, is visualising the effect of drinking alcohol, to questionably demonstrate whether prostate cancer can be avoided by giving up the excessive drinking of alcohol. Can prostate cancer happen to some men who do not drink alcohol at all? Is that point relevant, or not? Is it appropriate that some people like me can get prostate cancer by drinking excessive amounts of alcohol, even for a very short duration? And what happens, if excessive drinking of alcohol is continued on diagnosis of prostate cancer? Does anyone know the answers? It is important to point out the seriousness of prostate cancer and massive effect prostate cancer can have on one's life.

Alcohol Alcohol Alcohol Alcohol Alcohol Alcohol
Alcohol Alcohol Alcohol Alcohol Alcohol
Alcohol Alcohol Alcohol Alcohol
Alcohol Alcohol Alcohol
Alcohol Alcohol
Alcohol
!!!!!!
!!!
!
Prostate Cancer?
Other Cancer?

The repetition of the word alcohol above is just meant to indicate what I think excessive drinking of alcohol temporarily did to my prostate.

I do know that drinking alcohol can increase the chance of one getting cancer but according to my own thought process, drinking alcohol in excess for a few months possibly gave me prostate cancer.

I have not had any medical training. However, I believe that I have discovered some things about prostate cancer that the professors, surgeons, consultants and doctors need to look into. I admit, I do not know if I am right or not, but I have come across a unique situation that led me to believe that what I am writing needs to be investigated.

My overall approach to my alcohol drinking has changed for the better. Knowing a very little about alcohol drinking as well as about prostate cancer, I have given up drinking alcohol altogether. Believe me, I do feel better about my life in general, as well!

It is known that there is a link between alcohol drinking and some people getting cancer. Is it possible that some people who drink a lot of alcohol may have a bigger chance of getting cancer? Here is a thought. If you cannot stop drinking alcohol, does it make sense to reduce the amount of alcohol you are drinking? It needs to be repeated that a doctor's advice must be heeded. How many people in the world can reduce the chance of getting prostate cancer, and live longer, better lives? How many people can reduce the chance of getting more severe prostate cancer, by reducing their alcohol intake? Can these thoughts be proved right, at all? The readers of this article need to ask for experts'/specialists' opinions.

Chapter 20

Happiness Index

If you were to ask Leo, the imaginary child/person, how happy would you like to be? He would say about eight out of ten, meaning about eighty percent.

Leo would be asked, why only eighty percent Leo, when you have a choice of hundred percent happiness in your life, why choose eighty percent?

Leo would say, ‘I do want about eighty percent happiness in my life. That gives me a chance to be humble. A chance to be modest. That gives me better understanding of happiness/sadness, in life. If I am happy all the time, I would value happiness less, as I would expect happiness to be there all the time. If I’m happy all the time, perhaps I would stop trying to better myself, all the time. If I get a big bout of sadness, I may not be able to cope with the sadness. Again, I have selected eighty percent, If I select ninety percent happiness, the same logic would apply."

It is very important that any person who needs help or finds difficulties in coping with life should consult a doctor and heed their advice.

A happiness index is explained here from Leo's perspective. It is certain that not most people would agree with everything being written here. You need to understand that something that makes one person happy may not make another person happy. But it is worthwhile looking at wide variations to help find a good way to live your life.

So whilst thinking aloud, Leo is stretching his imagination to just one character with three different, very bad habits. Leo says to himself, "Imagine just one character with three very bad habits to start with, to scale the imaginary happiness index?

So Leo imagines a fifty-year-old person with three very bad habits. What are the three bad habits? To understand Leo's point of view, there are some very good assumptions made here. This is all imaginary and so no one reading this should feel bad about themselves or someone around them. Leo wishes every one good luck as much as possible. When the imagination is being stretched it has, perhaps, limited boundaries, but the concepts are worth understanding.

So this imaginary fifty-year old person with three very bad habits is asked, "How happy are you with your life? What is your life happiness index?" This imaginary person responds that the happiness level in his life is just twenty percent. The imaginary person says that heavy cigarette smoking, heavy alcohol drinking, a very bad gambling habit, and a partner having left him because of his bad habits, have each taken about twenty percent of the happiness index out of his life. Four times twenty percent of 'happiness index' being lost adds up to eighty percent 'happiness index' lost.

The 'happiness index' lost or gained in amounts are assumed figures and all these can vary from person to person. In this case here, the monetary and health costs due to smoking cigarettes, has reduced his 'happiness index' level by twenty percent in his life. Another individual may count his loss of happiness index as as ten percent due to smoking cigarettes. A third option for someone else with a different perspective may well count it as a five percent increase in happiness index because that person thought it was great that the individual started smoking cigarettes.

Heart disease, cancer of the lungs and other potential health problems may take their toll in the future, because a person started smoking cigarettes! These factors need to be considered, because these are important issues. Heavy drinking of alcohol as a bad habit gives you potentially very bad liver conditions and potentially some form of cancer in future! And to add to all these, your career has not just remained stagnant, it has suffered setbacks. What employer would ensure a heavy cigarette smoker, heavy alcohol drinking person and very bad gambler good career development? That takes you to the discussion about the very bad gambling habits that this individual has. As is generally believed, many gambling addicts frequently lose more money to gambling than they ever win. All these very bad habits are also followed by failure on the partnership level. That has taken another twenty percent of happiness, off his life. The partner having left a long time prior, his badly broken finances takes it's toll. He is barely holding on to a very bad roof over his head. This individual is defeated in almost all ways.

People are generally not easily able to give up heavy cigarette smoking, heavy alcohol drinking, and indeed bad levels of gambling. So to put things in perspective, Leo would imagine the best possible things happening now for this person. At the age of fifty-two, this heavy cigarette smoking individual, has given up cigarette smoking. Yes, I know, this in general does not happen, in real life, but let's go along with the imaginary situation. So the heavy cigarette smoking is assumed to be gone. Does that mean the twenty percent good happiness index is returned to the individual? No it hasn't. After giving up heavy cigarette smoking, the happiness index that had dropped by twenty percent has just managed to be a replacement of ten percent. These are all imaginary twenty and ten percent happiness index figures being stated here. Some people may not agree with all these analyses or other people may imagine different percent figures. The important point here is to understand the concepts and perspectives to see if all these can help some people improve their lives. This individual cannot compete with someone good like Leo who has never smoked cigarettes in his life. So the assumed drop of twenty percent happiness index in the individual's life has barely recovered by ten percent, because he has given up smoking cigarettes. And the almost permanent visible legacy of heavy smoking of cigarettes is badly stained teeth which is not going to help for the rest of his life. The state of his teeth and gums is bad and will remain bad until maybe he can get some dental work done, which this person is assumed to be not keen on.

Yes, you are trying your best to understand 'figments of imagination'. Now Leo is going to stretch your imagination further, and you are going to imagine that this individual has given up drinking of alcohol altogether. Yes, giving up heavy alcohol drinking is not easy at all, and for some folks, it does not happen because these folks simply cannot give up heavy drinking. Has that returned the twenty percent happiness index that was lost due to heavy drinking of alcohol? Even if you are generous in your mind, barely ten percent happiness index is returned on a temporary basis. Why temporary, you may ask? Well, there are no guarantees that a person will stick with no alcohol drinking for life and may return to drinking alcohol. And what about the bad gambling habit that was referred to? Let Leo stretch your imagination further and say that this individual has given up gambling all together. Yes, it does not happen in some cases, as a bad gambling habit is not easy at all to give up. So let's imagine that ten percent on the happiness index has returned, because gambling has been given up by this individual.

So compared to Leo who is living on almost eighty percent happiness index, this individual has barely climbed to a fifty percent happiness index, as he was addicted to heavy cigarette smoking, heavy drinking of alcohol, and very bad gambling habits. So the lesson is very simple. Do not start cigarette smoking, heavy drinking of alcohol and very bad gambling habits as these are very difficult habits to give up. Even when you are able to give up these habits, the damage done previously as well as future possibility of returning to these bad habits will always remain. And considerable damage is already done to life, health and wealth. And what about the partner who left this person some time ago? That twenty percent happiness index is, perhaps, gone for ever. So why not live a good life that may be possible if you do not go anywhere near these bad addictive habits.

And the list goes on. Too much spending money, too much of being a show-off, becoming too angry without control, and the biggest disaster, taking drugs, are not bad habits worth having. The big question is, do you want to live a good life like imaginary Leo?

Chapter 21

Happiness

Ha, Ha, Ha. It is catching isn't it? You keep on hearing someone laughing Ha__ Ha__ Ha__ for a while, you can't help but laugh, in most circumstances. Happiness, in the main comes from inside yourself, or more appropriately, 'from your heart'. If you are happy from the inside, it is very easy to bring the happiness to outside. You could be a catalyst for bringing joy, bringing happiness to someone else.

Leo learnt to filter any (even the slightest) bad event from his life as much as possible. Any little bad thing that would happen around him, he learnt to almost forget, if that was not likely to hurt anyone else. If any event or occasion was likely to hurt Leo himself or anyone else, he would see if he could find a way to stop that bad thing happening to himself or anyone else. Not thinking about any negative events or matters meant that Leo reserved most of the space in his life for good things and happiness. That meant Leo was almost always thinking positively and acting positively. Reading about an earthquake or floods in another country in the news would make Leo sad for a few minutes but knowing that he could do nothing about it, he would soon forget about it.

Leo was very amused when he was told about the 'being happy get-together, old-age retired people, group'. There was a talk about how some people (a circle of friends) would meet in the park, at a set time. They met at, say, seven o'clock every morning just to form a circle and laugh together. Two or three of the group laughed louder and the rest followed with even louder laughs. When Leo was told about it, the immediate question he had was, "Why would they get together just to laugh?" If a group of people go for a walk from their homes in the mornings, get some fresh air and meet in the park, what is wrong in that? Some of the members of the group would walk briskly which would give them better exercise in the morning and hopefully improve their health. Additionally, this group of friends laughed loudly and made themselves happy. Any people passing near the group and seeing them laughing would generally laugh and walk away. They are very happy. Let them be happy. Good luck to them. The answer is that being happy, pretending to be happy, happy almost all the time and keeping a happy persona within reason, may be a good idea.

How about going back to the toddler age when imaginary Leo was toddler. Leo was very lively, very healthy and very good at fifteen months' of age. One day, his imaginary grandmother decided to play hide and seek with Leo. When Leo was just standing behind the grandmother, the grandmother could not see Leo. She would say, "Where is Leo? I can't see him. Where is Leo?" And Leo would present himself, loudly laughing and almost jumping in front of his grandmother. Leo had learnt to walk for a couple of months, but he would jump and laugh. This would carry on for a little while. Then, the grandmother would sometimes say, "I am coming to get you. I am coming to get you!" when Leo is about five feet away. The grandmother would pretend and run on the spot saying, "I am coming to get you. I am coming to get you!" Leo would laugh loudly and be very, very happy. Any time that the grandmother saw Leo, she would have a big smile on her face and he reciprocated, smiling. The grandmother saw Leo about fifteen and a half days a month. So generally speaking, Leo was a very happy baby, almost all the time. You would think that Leo would be more successful than average, for that reason.

What was interesting was that the more happiness Leo experienced per day, it normally resulted in better sleep at night. His behaviour and happiness was normally better at the nursery the following day as well. Leo was building a routine of happiness. Leo's imaginary grandmother also started on a slogan. "Leo happy, grandmother happy." "Grandmother happy, Leo happy." Every time grandmother said this, Leo laughed.

One of the good reasons for that could be that Leo's happiness was from the inside. Anyone doing anything in life can perhaps do it better if they are happier from the inside. Growing up and starting to fit in this world could be one of the toughest tasks and if you can do it being happier from the inside, you can do it a lot better. Leo was wonderfully happy as a child and it is believed that part of the reason he developed a wonderful life is because he was happy most of the time. This did not happen by accident, as most of the characteristics of happiness were taught to him by his parent/s and grandparents.

Leo's parent/s discussed a lot of basic things with Leo to learn at nursery school. Leo spent years in nursery school and he had to learn those things, being happy, almost all the time, as his parent/s had taught him. Leo had to learn to play safely with toys. Leo had to learn not to hurt other children or teachers at the nursery. Leo had to learn to eat properly. Leo had to learn to drink water as suggested by teacher from time to time. Leo had to learn the alphabet. Leo had to learn to count some numbers, and so on. Leo had to learn to behave, have naps at certain times and be good. Leo had to learn to potty train with joint efforts of his teachers and parent/s. Leo had to keep on learning to be happy. The parent/s and nursery school decided to give the following life cup to Leo as a nursery school-leaving present.

Happy Life Cup, Happy Life Cup, Happy Life Cup.
Happy Life Cup, Happy Life Cup
Leo's Happy Life Cup
Happy Life Cup
Life Cup
!!!!
!!
!
Leo's Nursery School Happy Life Cup

At the time, Leo was very, very happy, and proud of himself. He was proud of his parent/s. He was proud of his nursery school teachers. He was proud of his nursery school.

Leo could hardly wait to join the primary school, finish learning at primary school and get even bigger Primary School Life Cup. At the secondary school, a Life Cup is very important to Leo, but he could hardly wait and looked forward to finishing secondary school, and then finishing a good university education. He expected to earn a very good salary in his first job and he eventually does it. He is on the road to give himself the title, 'Winner, Happy Life Cup'!

Whilst doing something, it is a lot better if you can train your mind to learn to do some good things and enjoy them as fun. For Leo, reading good books is good fun. Doing good physical exercise is good fun. Earning good money every month is very good fun!

There are lots of different proposals, ideas and actions that are suggested to lead to possible good results. Any details used by individuals or elders or parents or carers or teachers or youngsters in this book are done so at those individuals' own risks. The author, publishers, translators or distributors of this book do not accept any legal or other liabilities.

One can learn to be happy doing good things, very well. You can train yourself not to be lazy.

You can train yourself to talk with others politely and respectfully. You can train yourself to live within your means. That brings additional good happiness. Living a happy life is a lot easier than living a sad life. A sad life does happen from time to time, but a happy life happens a lot more often!

Chapter 22

Understanding Selective Success With Appreciation

The efficiency of any adventure, when demonstrated with incredible success in whatever field, can potentially be replicated in real life. This book has nothing to do with metallurgy. That is only referred to here in the last chapter in these last few pages.

There are three sets of potential groups according to me, the author, who need to take keen interest in this last chapter. The first group belongs to all the readers of this book who want to possibly pursue twice as good a life that they may want to achieve for themselves and for their children. Fortunately, the children generally have a number of years for education and can work towards twice the good life that they may pursue under the parent/s' guidance. Looking at texts of incredible successes may well act as "Motivation

Lift" to see if you or your child can also exceed success milestones in your lives. The second group is potential employers in developed countries who may wish to consider my example who reduced castings defects by some two thousand percent in years around 1978/79, after gaining university degree in India. I did receive, not requested, one of the most complimentary letters perhaps any employer could write to an employee. The copy of the letter that I received is attached although it is noted that my address then, in 1979, has changed many times. The third group of people could be Indian universities qualified graduates and postgraduates who need to feel proud about the university degree that they received in India. It may well be that some potential employer may question the validity of the degree that was received in India. The employer may be politely asked to look at the last chapter of this book. Would that help, I wonder?

Art of finding competent good employees may need significant updating, in some cases. Graduates and postgraduate people from India are perhaps viewed on standards of education by some employers in developed countries with some reservations? Could this be because of some lack of trust on the quality of education in India? I, having been educated in India in 1970-77 in general, trust the good standards of university education in India, to be very good and consider myself as one of the best examples of that. I also point out that I am the author of this book which may give a lot of inspiration to someone who wants to achieve very good living. My university education in India not only gave me a lot of knowledge on my subjects, but also prepared me wonderfully well for industry work. I did very good work in my first real job in a foundry in United Kingdom. Could some potential employers in United Kingdom, Australia and other developed countries do a significant rethink once they have read this chapter. I did reduce defects in castings by approximately two thousand percent. With exceptions even at present, there are many graduates and postgraduate people qualified in India who cannot get jobs that they are well qualified to do. The perception of some potential employers are that they are not up to the required standard. It is possible that many graduate and postgraduate people qualified in India may have achieved a very good standard.

I qualified as Bachelor of Engineering (Metallurgy), a five year degree course in M. S. University Baroda, India in 1977, with First Class Distinction. When I came to United Kingdom, I made many tens of applications and could not get any interviews. One manager introduced to me by my brother offered me a job to become a labourer which I politely refused. After a number of months, I did go for an interview at a foundry in Newport, South Wales. I was offered a job to cover technical duties in the foundry and I started the job. I started working very hard at the foundry using my university courses gained knowledge and observing what was happening in the foundry as a matter of routine. I made a number of changes taking cooperation of the people working there with diplomacy and tact. In short, I was doing everything that I was supposed to do according to my knowledge and good work ethic. We were making a number of castings for paper producing industries including about ten feet high, hollow, ten-ton cylinders for paper making industries. Normally when a casting was made, it would take about two months before that casting would end up in the machine shop.

About three months after I started working there, the head of the machine shop came walking very quickly to my office asking me, “Suresh, what have you done?, What have you done”? I was surprised wondering if something had gone wrong! Looking at the surprise on my face, the head of the machine shop explained in the following manner. He said, “The paper that is made by ten-ton cylinders that we make, needs to be smooth without defects. When we machine the cylinders, we need to make a very smooth circumference surface. When we find a defect, we drill a hole in the cylinder. We put a plug into the whole and cut it smoothly before machining it to a very fine, smooth mirror-like surface. That is how you get very smooth paper that does not have imperfections or ridges. We used to have about two hundred defects on each ten-ton cylinder before your time. Once your technical expertise has come along, we find that casting defects in each cylinder is reduced to about nine or ten. Imagine very labour intensive machining costs of about two hundred defects per cylinder reduced to about nine or ten! You are saving our company a fortune in reduced machining costs. It is also noted that when machining costs for ten-ton cylinders are reduced substantially, they are also reduced for other castings that need machining. After that job, I worked in Westinghouse foundry again making lots of good castings. Subsequently, I worked as a qualified metallurgical engineer for another employer, making parts for helicopters and jet aeroplanes for some time. The unmistaken sight of jet engines are the blades that can be easily seen revolving in the round engine, at the front of the aeroplane. I used to make those blades for jet engines.

A rethink is required on Indian institutions qualified Engineers, Professionals and Scientists being recognised as competent professionals to do good work in United Kingdom, Australia and other developed countries for following reasons:

1) ISRO The Indian Space Research Organisation has proved with space craft and associated technologies how good the Scientists and Engineers from India can do

excellent work, like sending spacecraft to the moon.

2) Those who saw some details of G20 summit conducted in India around 8th September 2023 may well have seen the very high quality in which many important matters were conducted.
3) "Pursue Twice as Good a Life" book written by India qualified Engineer Mr Suresh Thakrar might show the way to and maybe help achieve Double the "Good Standard of Living" of your child and a crisp copy of the book could show the potential employer in developed country the proof about India qualified person. In the last chapter of the book Suresh Thakrar reduced ten-ton cylinder castings defects in United Kingdom foundry by some 2000%.
4) Many employers in United Kingdom, Australia and other developed countries frequently do not recognise Indian Universities Qualifications . Mr Suresh Thakrar's employers Black-Clawson International Limited gave a chance to work in their foundry in Newport Gwent

around year 1978 and within months, about ten tons cylinders castings defects got reduced by some two thousand percent. Please see the copy of the letter sent by Mr R A Chalcraft, the Works Director when Suresh left that company.

5) I believe standards in Indian Universities were very good in 1972-77 when I got qualified as Bachelor of Engineering (Metallurgy) with First Class Distinction from M. S. University Baroda. Now, the standards in Indian Universities are better, according to what I have been able to observe, as best as possible. I think many country's Employers need to selectively welcome India qualified people for employment, as best as possible.
6) By all means, test the quality of potential employees but please try to see the real potential of Indian Universities Qualified graduates and postgraduate people.

Possibly improving your standard of living by up to one hundred percent or more is massive, gigantic, phenomenal… if it can happen? Parents trying to improve the standard of living of children by up to a hundred percent or more in the future is massive, gigantic, phenomenal... if that can happen. The children have a number of years studying, where the time can be well spent preparing for perfection in improving their standard of living in the future. Whatever improvements are made to the standard of living; one can hope that that is good. Perhaps, you can keep on trying to improve your standard of living in the future. I want to thank you all for reading my book and wish you all, a very good future.

A copy of my employer's letter in year 1979 after I had left the company is shown on the next page. This book and that letter speaks volumes on the potential possibilities of substantial improvements in qualities of life for many people and youngsters.

Black-Clawson International Ltd.

July 23, 1979

Westgate Works,
East Dock Road,
Newport,
Gwent, NPT 2TT
United Kingdom.

Telephone
Newport 65441

Cables
Blaclawson Newport

Telex 49335

Mr. S.J. Thakrar,
11 Ellfield Court,
Lings,
Northampton,
NN3 4LR

Dear Suresh,

I was extremely sorry to hear of your decision to leave the Company, however, I can well understand your reason for coming to this decision. You have made an excellent contribution to the successful operation of our Iron Foundry in the last few years.

On behalf of the staff, the foundry personnel and myself I want to take this opportunity of wishing you and your wife every happiness and success in the future.

Yours truly,

R.A. CHALCRAFT
WORKS DIRECTOR

c.c. Mr. A. Scotson
Mr. K. Cook

RAC/KH/1362

Directors: C. C. Landegger (USA) Chairman R. A. Chalcraft (Canada) Sir Robert Clark A. Kershaw G. F. Landegger (USA) E. C. Langdon P. D. Mosher (Canada) N. D. Root (Managing) J. B. Scott, C.B.E. D.F.C. D. F. Todd

Registered Number: 462306 England Registered Address: 20-26 Wellesley Road, Croydon, Surrey CR9 2BR Telex 946323 Telephone 01-686-3399